ZOMPOC SURVIVOR:

ODYSSEY

For Kate & Ron

BEN REEDER

Thanks!

Ben Reeder

Zompoc Survivor: Odyssey

Copyright © 2015 Ben Reeder

Cover art: Angela Gulick

Other books by Ben Reeder:
The Demon's Apprentice series:
The Demon's Apprentice
Page of Swords

The Zompoc Survivor series:
Zompoc Survivor: Exodus
Zompoc Survivor: Inferno
Zompoc Survivor: Odyssey

Also from Irrational Worlds:

The Wormwood Event (Free)

The Dossiers of Asset 108
Rationality Zero
The Primary Protocol

Dave's Rules of Survival

1. 98% of survival is mental. Attitude, knowledge and planning ahead will keep you alive when shit hits the fan.
2. Only 2% of survival is physical, but it's an important 2%.
3. Rule of three: 3 minutes without air, 3 hours without shelter, 3 days without water, 3 weeks without food.
4. Plan ahead.
5. Always have a back up for everything. Have a Plan B, because Plan A almost never works.
6. Keep the basics for survival with you at all times.
7. Know your terrain.
8. Always carry a sharp knife.
9. Always know where the exits are and know how to get to them in a hurry and in the dark.
10. Always make sure you know where your clothes and your gear are, and be able to get to them in the dark.
11. Have at least two sources of light at all times.
12. Assume that people suck after shit hits the fan, and that they're after your stuff.
13. Don't be one of the people who suck after shit hits the fan.
14. Guns are not magic wands. If you point one at someone, don't assume they're going to automatically do what you tell them to. Be ready to pull the trigger if they don't.
15. Assume every gun is loaded if you're not in a fight. Don't point a gun at anything you want to keep.
16. Don't count on any gun you might pick up during a fight. There might be a very good reason it's on the ground.
17. Never put your finger on the trigger until you're ready to pull it. Be sure of your target and what's behind it if you do.
18. Know how shit works.
19. Never assume you know enough. Assume you always need to learn more.
20. If shit hasn't hit the fan, it isn't too late to prepare.
21. Always try your plan and gear out before you rely on it to keep you alive.
22. Watch out for your friends and family. No part of your survival prep is more important.
23. Don't walk away if you can help.

From the Journal of Maya Weiss
October 26, 2013

Between the traffic jams and avoiding the zombies, it's been really slow going. Cars were backed up on the highway between Kansas City and Denver, and the side roads weren't much better. We made it into Nebraska today, which means we probably averaged less than ten miles per hour after we left Fort Riley. I'm not in a big hurry to get to Wyoming as long as Dave and Amy are behind me.

Porsche's been spending a lot of time with Mike, the Marine corporal who was flirting with her back in Nevada. She tried to sneak back into the truck last night, but I was still up. She tried to apologize, and when I asked her why, she stuttered and then clammed up, just like a teenage girl trying to be tactful about walking in on you and your boyfriend making out. But when I asked her to tell me about Mike, she started talking again. I guess after things get settled again, he's going to be a truck driver. He has it in his head that traveling between groups of survivors is going to be something that will be at a premium for a long time. I guess he has a point.

After she crawled into her bunk, I stayed up and listened to the shortwave for a while. It's a mixed bag out there.

Radio Concho, out of San Angelo: A mix of music in both Spanish and English, and a daily kill report. Evidently, there is a competition between three hunter teams for most zombies killed. One team is a historical reenactment group called the Buffalo Soldiers, the second is the Rams, from the athletics department from the local college and the third is the One Three Knights, a local gang that became part of the Fort Concho group. So far the Buffalo Soldiers are in the lead but the One Three Knights are catching up.

Radio Free America, out of St Louis: "The People's Choice for News and Music" "President" Shaw is a regular here. Lots of slick, patriotic music; deep baritone voice-over; nothing positive reported. They do a lot of blaming everyone else for "the problems this country is facing" and claim President Shaw is the man to get things done. Tonight, they talked about the "freedom strike" in Kansas City again, and the heroic efforts of

Daniel, a Christian leader who has saved countless lives and evidently killed a million zombies with his bare hands or something. According to them, Dave is a socialist trying to live on Daniel's hard work but refusing to contribute to it himself. I'll have to ask Dave about the whole socialist thing when I see him again. To hear them tell it, Dave abducted all the women in the new Eden complex, then ran off and joined some sort of socialist commune that stole the bread right out of the mouths of the hundred tiny babies Daniel was himself nursing back to health...when he wasn't killing zombies, raising the dead and single-handedly saving the world. What bullshit. What's troubling is that they suspect Dave was killed by the strike, but they're saying that it isn't confirmed. Which means they might still be looking for him.

Radio Z: This one is hard to pin down. Some nights he's on, some nights he's not. I think he's mobile, because a lot of times, he just says "Transmitting to you from the heart of the wasteland" before he starts talking. He calls himself Johnny Apocalypse. Tonight, he said he was on top of a water tower, and that he could see for miles. Then, he stopped in the middle and said "Do you hear that?" In the silence that followed, I could hear a train blowing its horn in the distance. "That, ladies and gentlemen, is the sound of hope calling out to us from the dark of the night after the end of the world, calling us to follow it toward the dawn." He has a poet's soul. He played "City of New Orleans", then some Bob Dylan and ended with Three Doors Down's 'Citizen Soldier'. Before he signed off, he said he was heading north. "There's a town I heard about that's having some troubles so I'm gonna go walk the ground around it and listen to the wind. Who knows...maybe there's a hero or two left out there."

The answer my friend is blowin' in the wind...

Chapter 1
Road Trip
~ *"All journeys have secret destinations of which the traveler is unaware"* ~

Martin Buber

Highway 40 out of Kansas City was packed with cars and dead people, some more dead than others. If a divided four lane was this bad, I wasn't even going to try to imagine what Interstate 70 was like. With the rain still coming down in thick drops, the more active corpses couldn't seem to make sense of things unless we got within a few yards of them. The first time one stumbled across out path, I smeared him across the front bumper of the truck. At least, I think it was a him. The second time, we were navigating around the wreck of a semi that had turned on its side when we found ourselves a few feet away from a group of deadheads munching on the bloated remains of the cattle that had been the truck's cargo. Amy yelled out a warning, and I hit the gas. On rain slick roads in a five mile long traffic jam, that wasn't the smartest thing I'd done all day. We ended up turned sideways, and the truck stalled. Immediately, I tried to restart it. After a few seconds, I stopped though. I wasn't getting anywhere, and I figured the infected would be close to the truck by then. But when I looked out the window, I saw them wandering around only a few feet closer to us.

"What are they doing?" Amy asked. She was a pretty sharp kid, so I looked closer. After a few seconds of watching, I noticed it too. Most of the time, the zombie walk was a slow shuffle with the hands at the side. If there was food nearby, the arms came up and the fingers curled like claws to grab anything with a pulse and drag it toward the mouth. This group had their arms up, but they didn't have the forward reach going on. Instead, they were moving their arms back and forth in front of them. As I stared, the sky lit up for the umpteenth time that morning, and thunder hit like a fist, rattling the truck's windows. The zombies started and then began moving in a different direction.

"They're blind," I said softly. "The rain, the thunder and the lightning…the higher functions that help us sort that kind of thing out must not work in the infected. At least not in the dead ones."

"No bets on it working on the ghouls, huh?" Amy asked.

"I wouldn't bet my life on it," I said. The truck started on the second try, and I pulled back onto the shoulder of the road. The shoulder wasn't much better since every few yards we found where someone else had the same idea but with more fatal results.

"We've got to get off the highway," Amy said when we passed a turnoff.

"I'm looking for a roadblock," I told her as I pulled around a gutted minivan. "I still need a new gun." The wheels slipped in the grass on the side of the road and I let off on the gas to let the truck coast a little ways before I pulled back onto the loose asphalt.

"I thought you loved the Ruger." She pointed to the little 10/22 Takedown that was stowed behind me.

"I do, and if I had to take just one gun, that's the one I'd choose. But I like having something a little bigger around, too." I pulled around the wreck of a little red compact car and drove along the shoulder for another half mile before we came to an overpass. On the far side, a stretch of clear road beckoned beyond the on ramp. I inched my way between two parked cars and crossed the grass median that separated the ramp from the access road, and we were on rough asphalt.

The access road followed the highway for a few hundred yards, far enough for us to get past the concrete barricades that had been set across the road two deep. Disappointed, I crossed the grass to get back on the highway, and a couple of miles later, we drove out from under the rain right before the road turned south. After a week and a half under the smoke that blanketed Kansas City, sunlight was a welcome sight, but I almost missed the rain and the added cover it lent. Still, sunshine was sunshine, even during October. We rolled the windows down and let the sun warm us up. Even in dry clothes, I still felt a little damp after swimming across the Kansas River, and I caught sight of Amy's hands shaking a few times. She'd snagged a pair of gray camo pants and a hoody at one of the stores in Wyandotte Plaza, but the hoodie and the t-shirt weren't enough to dispel the chill. I couldn't blame the icy sensation that still ran down my back entirely on the weather, though. Swimming across the Kansas River had been more like swimming the River Styx to escape Hell. We'd left a lot of demons behind in KC, and very few of them were the strictly metaphorical kind. A little sunshine was welcome in more ways than one.

I saw what I was looking for as we passed a line of trees and found ourselves looking out across an open field. Parked on an overpass south of us were a Humvee and what looked like a Bradley Fighting Vehicle. The road going east from there was clear. I couldn't see the other side, but I was pretty sure it was crammed with cars all the way back into Lawrence. Ahead, I could see the sign for Kansas Highway 9 as it crossed 40, and I took the left turn. Almost immediately, I could see the overpass and the Bradley's turret pointed west. We passed a couple of quiet little farms, and I did my best to keep my eyes on the road. I didn't want to see what might be looking out of the windows of those houses. The bigger question in my head was which I was more frightened of seeing, the living or the dead. The first I'd want to stop and try to help, and the second would just haunt me as my writer's imagination conjured up what might have happened behind the doors of those houses.

Nothing or no one rushed out toward us as we got closer to the overpass, and I slowed down and pulled to the left side of the road. Amy looked at me with one eyebrow raised as I put the truck in park looked toward Lawrence. Vehicles were backed up as far as I could see, but nothing moved. Two weeks of surviving the zombie apocalypse had taught me a lot about the undead, and one was that the mostly dead ones, stage two infected if you wanted a clinical name for them, tended to stay close to where they died until they had a good reason to move on. In some cities they followed the survivors who got out. Springfield's city limits had been pretty porous, but Kansas City had been bordered by a river on the west side, so a lot of them had backed up against the few bridges that military hadn't bombed to rubble. Lines of cars meant oceans of dead people who hadn't got the message. Lawrence struck me as being pretty damn open. It was in freaking *Kansas*, after all. No road? No problem. Just drive over the flattest fields in the U.S. This whole area should have been

9

crawling with infected. But we hadn't seen a walker for a few miles.

"Let me guess," Amy snarked from beside me. "You've got a bad feeling about this."

"The Farce is strong in you, padawan," I said as I undid my seatbelt. "Do you?" She closed her eyes for a few seconds, then opened them and shook her head. It was a reminder of one of the things I hadn't quite gotten used to, an ability to sense the undead that we shared. Amy was a lot better at it than I was, but she was more comfortable with it, too.

"I don't *feel* anything," she said after a moment. "Not for a while. Is that what's got you spooked?" I nodded and opened the truck door. She got out as I did and held up her Ruger. "I've got your six," she said, trying to sound casual.

"Aim for the neural strip, the T in the face if you have a forward facing zombie. Eyes, nose, mouth," I gestured at my own face as an example. "If they're looking to one side...well, you already know the best targets there."

"I do?" she asked. Her eyebrows went up a little, giving the grin on her face a sort of surprised look.

"Same place you shot the Necromancer," I said as I pulled receiver and barrel for the Ruger Takedown from its pack. "Temple and ears. Keep your eyes off your scope until you have a target. And don't try to shout at me or get my attention. Shoot first, let the shot warn me. I'll get the message." The slide went back under my thumb and I pressed the locking tab to hold it in place. Inserting the barrel into the receiver was only a few seconds' worth of work, and it clicked into place with a twist. Unlike my standard model 10/22, I'd grabbed four Ruger BX-25 magazines for the Takedown. Without a scope on it, I wasn't expecting to be doing a whole lot of precision shooting. Not that I was a bad shot with iron sights, but I was a whole lot better with a scope. Hence the need for less time reloading between missed shots. With the Takedown assembled, I put the pack back on and loaded a magazine, then released the slide and flipped the rear sights up.

Under Amy's sights, I headed to my left and made for the eastern side of the overpass. Once I got to the road, I could see that the Bradley was blocking the right lane on the bridge, with a

Humvee taking up the left lane. Between the two, they effectively owned the entire road. The back ramp of the Bradley was down, which made me stop for a second. At a roadblock, I would have figured standing orders were to be buttoned up tight. The Humvee's doors looked like they were all closed, but as I got within a few feet, the rear door on the driver's side opened a few inches as a breeze picked up and ruffled my hair. The Ruger came up by reflex, and I waited to see if anything else happened. After a few seconds, I lowered the rifle and crept a little closer. More details started to stand out to me with every step. There was no gun in the pintle mount on the Humvee, and the Bradley's top hatches were standing open, letting light stream down into the vehicle. The underside of the Humvee was visible as I came further up the incline, showing nothing but daylight between the road and the chassis. I wished hard for a scope on the Ruger, but nothing came of it, just like always.

Brass littered the ground between the two vehicles, and I could see bullet holes and burn damage on the cars closest to the roadblock. As I drew close the Bradley, I could see why it wasn't buttoned up. The interior was blackened from fire damage, and I could see the melted shapes of electronics in the turret. That usually meant the vehicle's position had been overrun, and they'd popped thermite to keep it from being captured intact. Fighting every instinct I had, I scurried up between the two vehicles and poked my head up to look in the Humvee. The inside was blackened as well, evidence of another thermite charge. My shoulder blades tried to pull together as I climbed the side of the Bradley and crouched behind the turret. To the west, I could see the line of cars stretching back toward Lawrence. A lake took up most of the left side of the road, stretching an easy six or seven hundred yards to the west. I stayed on the side opposite the lake. If I was going to hang out anywhere right now, a place with a supply of water nearby seemed like the perfect place. Then it hit me, what had been bothering me about this whole place.

No bodies. Since zompoc Monday, I'd seen hard core Special Forces soldiers leave comrades where they'd fallen if they were bitten. I'd watched Marines burn their dead on the roof of a hospital to make sure they didn't get up and follow us. No one took chances with bodies any more. If any of the troops in the Bradly or the Humvee had fallen, either to zombies or to angry villagers with torches and hunting rifles, I should have seen bodies. Thermite burned hot, but I knew it didn't burn long enough to completely reduce a body to ash. It was one of the less savory things running around in my head and I was pretty sure the NSA had tagged it in my search history. For that matter, I didn't see any bodies on the road. No suitcases or storage containers on top of cars. No zombies. Thousands of bullet holes peppered every car in my line of sight, and lots of blood covered the ground in dark patches, but the kill zone in front of me was devoid of bodies.

A shudder ran through me at the thought of what might have happened to the dead, followed closely by a colder dose of fear as I asked myself another question. *Who has the soldiers' weapons?* The thought had barely registered before my feet hit asphalt again, and I was running toward the guard rail. My left hand propelled me over the metal rail and my feet hit the uneven ground hard enough to sink into the soft turf and keep me from tumbling down the hill. Amy kept her eyes on the road behind me until I opened the door and jumped behind the wheel. As soon as the engine turned over, she was in the passenger seat and hitting the safety on her rifle. She had barely buckled herself in when I put the truck in reverse and hit the gas. I didn't try to turn around on the little one lane road. Instead I just kept going for the three hundred yards between our butts and the nearest driveway. My rear bumper took out part of the split rail fence as I cut sharp into the gravel drive and hit the brakes, then shifted into gear. Rocks sprayed the lawn behind me as I hit the gas again, and I took out the mailbox before I hit the road again.

"Dave, what is it?" Amy asked as she looked back behind us. "What did you find?"

"Nothing," I said as I blew through the four way intersection. "Way too much nothing. No bodies, no stuff."

"They'd been looted already?" she asked. I shook my head.

"No, they'd been taken. All of them. I didn't see a pyre, and I can only think of one reason to take bodies right now if you're not gonna burn 'em." My voice sounded a lot calmer than I felt.

In my peripheral vision, I could see Amy's face go slack as she followed my train of logic, then she grimaced.

"You can't be serious," she said. I sped past a school and kept my natural reflexes in check for all of six seconds before I replied.

"I'm very serious," I said. "And don't call me Shirley." She rolled her eyes at the lame movie quote, but her head turned to look behind us again. The road curved ahead of us, and I followed it left, opting to go west as far as I could. It kept edging west, and I kept the gas pedal as close to the floor as I dared. Up ahead I could see where the road doglegged, and I cut the edge as close as I dared, relieved to see a sign for Kansas 59 a mile ahead. As soon as we hit 59, I floored it again, heedless of how much fuel I might be burning. It wasn't like I needed to worry about the price of gas.

"We need to pass north of Topeka," I told Amy as I pulled a Kansas map from the glove compartment. "And if we can find another town, maybe we'll find a roadblock we can check."

"Where the hell are we?" she asked as she tried to unfold the map.

"North of Lawrence on 59. We just passed an airfield back there." Her finger hovered over the map for a moment, then dropped to the paper.

"Got it. Stay on this when it goes north and then back west...there's a little town called Perry not far ahead."

"Yeah," I said drily. "About four miles, according to the sign."

"Smartass," she said. I didn't bother to tell her to mind her language. Post ZA, being a good father figure to a teen seemed to be more about teaching her survival skills and less about manners or social niceties. So far, I thought I was doing a pretty good job. We were both still alive, and after getting out of KC in one piece, that was saying something. I still wanted my damn "World's Deadliest Dad" coffee mug.

The road was pretty clear, with only the occasional car wreck to break up the scenery. Most of those were off the road, with the cars either wrapped pretty solidly around trees or telephone poles. We passed one field where a truck had gone off-roading into a thousand acres of freshly turned dirt. The tracks arced gently toward the only thing for a dozen square miles: a bright green combine. The truck's front end was lost under the combine's thresher blades, its rear wheels off the ground. A mile further on, we had to slow down and swerve around a head on collision between a dark blue minivan and a silver BMW. I tried not to look, but I saw movement in both vehicles from the corner of my eye. I wondered how many ghouls and zombies were trapped forever in dead vehicles by the simple barrier of a fastened seatbelt. When the road turned back west, we found ourselves on what looked like the border between Kansas and the rest of the US. On our right, the northern side of the road was dominated by low hills and trees, while the southern side was all open fields and flat as Kansas was known to be.

Less than ten minutes later, I saw what I had been hoping for. Up ahead was a white sheriff's patrol car. Unfortunately, it was surrounded by infected. I slowed and pulled to the left about a hundred yards away. I made the count about twenty, maybe a few more. Beside me, Amy was bouncing in her seat.

"Can I take care of them?" she asked, the words tumbling out of her mouth.

"Remember, aim for the face, not the forehead," I said as I opened the door. From my side of the truck, I watched as she steadied her rifle against the door and took careful aim. A crack split the air, and one of the infected fell. I heard her exhale and then she fired again. None of the zombies dropped, and she cursed, then pulled the trigger again. This time one fell. Slowly, the infected turned toward us, and she put another one down. After she dropped three more of them, they started our way. One broke from the shambling walk of the dead into a trot, then a sprint.

"I'll get the runner," I said as I pressed the safety and leveled the Takedown at it. "You keep busting heads." I put the bead in the middle of its blue button up shirt and pulled the trigger. A dark splotch appeared just to the left of the button line, but the ghoul kept coming. I pulled the trigger five more times, and all I did was mess up its wardrobe. The .22 rounds weren't killing it fast enough, so I tossed the Ruger on the seat and drew the SOCOM from the tactical holster on my right leg, cursing my still wet vest in the back of the cab as I worked the slide. Left

14

handed, I was a decent shot with a pistol. Right handed, my only saving grace was the SOCOM's Laser Aiming Module. The green dot bounced around on the ghoul's torso, and I stroked the trigger. The shot went wide, and I aimed to the left, knowing my tendency was to twitch to my gun hand side when I pulled the trigger. The second round caught the ghoul high and on the right, sending it spinning to that side before it hit the ground. I took the brief moment to change hands, and when it scrambled to its feet, I put the green LAM dot on its chest and fired two more times. Both shots hit it just to the right of the breastbone, and it fell on its butt. For a moment, it just looked at me, it chest heaving as blood coated its body. Then its head wobbled and it fell back to the road.

Beside me, the steady crack of Amy's Ruger paused as she slid a fresh magazine home. There was a click as she released the bolt and a heartbeat later, she pulled the trigger again. As she fired, I holstered the SOCOM and grabbed the Takedown from the seat. By now, almost half of the infected were down. I leveled the bead on the Ruger's barrel on the nose of one of the infected and pulled the trigger. To my surprise, it dropped like a puppet with the strings cut. Not a bad shot at fifty or sixty yards.

"Hey!" Amy protested.

"Keep shooting," I told her. "It's not a contest." Still, I only dropped three more in the time it took her to take care of another nine. "Good shooting," I told her as I slid behind the wheel again. My heart grew a couple of sizes when she smiled at the compliment and seemed to mean it when she said "Thanks."

"I see why you want a bigger gun," she added as we drove up on the cruiser. I stopped about ten yards away and did a careful U-turn using the little side road to the left of the road so that the truck's tailgate was facing the sheriff's car, then backed the rest of the way, rolling over a couple of bodies along the way. The stench hit as the wind shifted, and I got out of the truck wishing for more rain or a little bit stronger wind, say something on the order of an F1 tornado. I heard Amy gag on the smell as we walked toward the cruiser. Once I cleared the rear of the truck, I squatted down to check under the patrol car and saw nothing but daylight. Amy brought her rifle up and scanned the double line

15

of cars that stretched back toward Perry. She lowered it and gave me a thumbs up a few moments later.

The driver's side door was open, and the deputy's bloated body was in the seat with the seatbelt buckled. An AR-15 was on the ground beside him, the magazine well empty. His pistol was on the floorboard, and I could see several bloody bite marks on his hands and arms. More telling was the gaping hole in the top of his head, and the smaller hole under his chin. I swallowed down the taste of bile in my mouth and started the business of stripping what I could from him. His service belt used Velcro instead of a buckle, and I thanked any deity that would listen for that. Once I had the belt and his pistol, I grabbed the keys from the ignition and stepped back, fighting hard just to keep yesterday's dinner down. The radio was useless, so I pulled it from the belt and tossed it into the car before I walked around to the other side. The passenger seat yielded a duty bag that held a change of uniform, a second pistol and two boxes of ammo for it and a few other bits of gear. I grabbed it and went to the trunk.

On most patrol cars, the trunk was a mobile supply depot, and this one was no different. A Mossberg 500 Law Enforcement model was locked into the rack at the back of the trunk, and several plastic tackle and tool boxes filled the rest of the space. I did a quick visual check of them, finding crime scene gear, a digital camera, binoculars and crime scene tape in one box, and a first aid kit, emergency blankets and a fire extinguisher in another. I grabbed both boxes and put them in the truck bed, then came back and grabbed the guns and ammo. A duffel bag had water, a couple of MREs and some energy bars inside, which I grabbed along with the regular tool box. Lastly, I grabbed the defibrillator and jump box. On my last trip to close the trunk, I picked up the mesh bag with a trio of stuffed animals in it. The only things left were the traffic vest, a set of spike strips and a box of blank forms by the time I closed the trunk.

"Dave," Amy said as I closed the tailgate and shell top. Her eyes were on the road behind us. Sunlight glinted off the windshield of a vehicle, and I could see the headlight from a motorcycle. Whether it was my potential cannibal horde or another group of people, I had no idea. What I was sure of was that I didn't want them following us. I ran back to the patrol car.

"Get in the truck!" I yelled to Amy as I popped the trunk open and grabbed the spike strips. My feet couldn't seem to move me fast enough as I sprinted for the door of the truck. Once again, I spun the tires when I put the truck in gear. The rear end fishtailed as I made a hard right turn and went cross country until I hit the side road that ran west, straight toward Perry. I stopped about thirty yards down the road and got out to spread the spike strip across the cracked asphalt, spending seconds I didn't really feel like I had. Once I was back behind the wheel, I breathed a little easier.

"Are they…?" Amy almost asked.

"Cannibals? Don't know. After us? Maybe. We'll know if they try to follow us. Right now, I need you to crawl in the back and grab the pistol and as many magazines as you can for me, then I need you to load the shotgun." I risked a glance in the rearview mirror, but the other vehicles still hadn't made it to the turn off.

"On it," Amy said as she crawled over the seat and through the opening in the rear window into the truck bed. A few seconds later, she leaned across the back of the seat with the pistol in hand. "There were only a couple of shots left in the magazine in it, so I loaded the last one in it. There's a round in the chamber." I took the gun with a nod and she pushed herself back into the camper shell. With nothing but straight road ahead of me for half a mile, I took the chance to see what I was shooting. The boxy design was characteristic of a Glock, and sure enough, when I turned it to look at the left side, I saw the trademark Glock brand and the number 22 engraved on the slide, with .40 to the right of that. I hadn't had much experience with the .40 Smith and Wesson, but Nate had spoken highly of it. I set the Glock down and drew the SOCOM, remembering that I'd fired four rounds from it. Keeping one eye on the road, I dropped the mag out of it and pulled a fresh one from the tactical holster. With a full mag and a round in the chamber on both pistols, I had twenty nine rounds to hand without having to reload. I hoped it would be more than enough. While I was hoping, I went for broke and hoped I didn't have to use either gun.

My optimism died a quick death as I saw movement in the rearview mirror. The bike swerved and kept coming, but two cars behind it didn't look so lucky. The first one swerved left but the second one just kept going straight across the strip. A third car went the opposite way, and I wasn't sure if it managed to clear the spikes or not. Either way, I was pretty sure at least one of them wasn't going to catch up to us. We were coming up on an intersection, and I looked along the road crossing it by habit. Both sides were clear, but a railroad crossing on my left caught my attention. It factored into my plans as I thought that over. Railroads didn't just stop in small towns. They usually went straight through them, which meant there was probably at least one road on this side of town that ended up running right alongside it. If I could find it, I had a route all the way through Perry.

The blue roof of the car wash that stood on one corner of the intersection was a blur on my left as I sped through the stop sign, and I heard the buzz of a street bike behind me. Trees lined the left side of the road on the far side of a shallow drainage ditch as we sped past the intersection and into the edge of town. The bike's buzz became a muted roar as it sped up and came around on my side. I caught my first glimpse of the rider, all black leather with a helmet that only left his eyes visible. For a moment, it settled in my side mirror as the rider drew a sawed off shotgun from a holster on his hip. My right hand fell on the Glock and I brought it up to my chest. The rider twisted the throttle and drew up beside me, lifting the shotgun as he came.

It was a tactic that had probably worked several times before, drawing up beside some unsuspecting driver and just unloading both barrels before they could react. It relied on surprise and reluctance in other people to shoot first. Neither was the case now, and the look on the rider's face when I pulled the trigger was probably the same expression he was used to seeing on the other side of the gun. I fired several times and watched his body jerk twice as I got really lucky. He veered off to the left, then disappeared from view when he hit a parked car.

"Dave, we've got one behind us!" Amy called out from the rear of the truck. No sooner had the words left her mouth than the truck jerked from impact. Behind me, I could hear Amy cursing, then I heard the camper shell's rear window opening. The Mossberg boomed, and the car behind us, a late model red

Mustang, swung into view in my side mirror. Its front windshield was starred and white around a hole the size of a dinner plate almost dead center in the glass.

"Aim for the front grill next!" I yelled over my shoulder. She didn't respond, but I heard the shotgun boom three more times in rapid succession, and the next time I saw the Mustang, it was stopped in the middle of the road with steam billowing from the hood. Then the first figures ran out from the houses on the left, and I looked to the road ahead. I couldn't honestly say I felt bad about leaving them to their fate, but it wasn't one I felt like watching. It also wasn't one I felt like making Amy watch.

"Good shooting," I called out to her. "Close up the window and come back up front. I need your help getting out of town." The road merged ahead and I followed it west across an old truss bridge over the Delaware River as she slid into the rear part of the cab.

"Looks like that whole getting out of town thing pretty much just happened," she said.

"We need to head north, and get away from the railroad tracks," I told her as I handed her the map. "We have places to be…and to not be."

"Where to be or not to be, that is the question," she said.

Chapter 2
Rule 23

*~ Yes, how many times can a man turn his head/Pretending
he just doesn't see?~*
Bob Dylan, "Blowin' In the Wind"

"I've never shot anyone before," Amy said over her dinner.

"I'm pretty sure you still haven't," I said after I swallowed
the bite of fried Spam I'd just taken.

"Are you quoting Firefly lines at me, or are you serious?" For
all that she was troubled, her appetite wasn't suffering any. She
had finished the Spam and spooned the last of the corn from the
can she'd just taken off the fire onto her mess kit plate.

"Not intentionally," I said. "I mean it, I think you scared them
more than anything with that first shot. There will come a time
when you're going to have to shoot someone, though." I watched
her face as I set the Kelly Kettle on the base and dropped a few
twigs and leaves down through the chimney. The little fire inside
blazed up and showed me the frown that creased her brow.

"How do you deal with it?" she asked. Gone was the
enthusiasm she'd shown that afternoon for shooting zombies. I
looked around the barn we were in, remembering how fast she'd
been in nailing the ghoul that had rushed us as we pulled into the
farmstead. Then she hadn't hesitated. If she was going to
survive, she needed to be ready to pull the trigger just as fast
with a living person when the moment called for it.

"I know what I'm willing to die for," I said after a few
moments of thought. "Once you know that, you know what
you're willing to kill for, and you can make peace with it."

"Sounds too simple," she said.

"Simple doesn't mean easy. I don't like hurting people; it
bugs the hell out of me. But if someone is trying to kill me or my
people, they're going to get the same right back." I stood up and
went to the tailgate of the truck, not sure I wanted her to see my
face just then. When I had to think about it, I was less sure about
what I'd done today. In my head, I'd already convicted the man
I'd shot of who knows how many crimes, when all I really knew
was that he pointed a shotgun at me. I had imagined him
shooting other drivers before me, and assumed he liked it. I had
assumed the worst of him, and I'd been completely confident I

21

was right. Rule Twelve was pretty simple: *Assume people suck after shit hits the fan, and that they're after your stuff.* I had created the next rule to counter the tendency to become that kind of person: *Don't be one of the people who suck after shit hits the fan.* But was I telling myself I was following one rule to justify killing people with the other? I looked back over my shoulder at Amy.

Suddenly, everything was clear as day, just as it had been when I pulled the trigger. They were trying to kill me. And if they had succeeded, they would have tried to do worse to Amy when they found her. And I would give my own life to keep her from that fate. It was that simple. Of course, if I ever did have to give my life for hers, I wasn't going to make it easy. The man who tried to take my life was going to pay dearly for the effort. I reached into the duffel back and pulled out the small plastic bag I'd found earlier while we were taking care of the guns. Inside were five little pieces of plastic that could be clipped to a belt loop or a hem. I pulled two out and went back to the overturned milk crates we were using as stools.

"Clip one of those to your back belt loop, and put the other one in your front pocket," I told her as I held my hand out. She cupped her palm under my hand to catch them, and I demonstrated by clipping one of my own to my rear belt loop.

"What are they?" she asked as she looked them over.

"Handcuff keys. Some cops carry them to keep from being locked up with their own cuffs." She wasted no time in tucking one to her belt loop, and I stuck the second one in my front pocket.

"You don't already have some of these?" she asked with a smug little grin on her face.

"Nope," I said. "Before things went south, I wouldn't carry them. I didn't want to give the police the wrong impression if I ever had to deal with them. But…things change." She nodded. By then the water in the Kelley kettle was boiling, and I took it off the base and poured some into the small pot that came with the kettle's cook set. Three minutes later, I had Ramen noodle soup.

"So, what's the plan now?" she asked after I finished my soup and headed back to the truck.

"We find an encrypted radio and contact Nate. After that, we wing it."

"Oh, is that all we have to do?" Amy said sharply. "Let me check, I think I had an encrypted radio around here somewhere. Dave, seriously, where the hell are we going to find one?"

"National Guard armory," I said as I picked up the AR-15 and hit the power button on the red dot sight. The little illuminated circle glowed into existence, and I turned the power off before I set it down. "Or, if we're lucky, we might find a convoy or some kind of mobile command post." The AR had two mags, just enough to get me into serious trouble. The shotgun was a little better off, with a hundred shells. Since they didn't require a magazine to load, that wasn't so bad. The Glock only had the two mags, which meant I would probably have to rely more on the SOCOM than I would have liked, since I had fewer rounds for it. The only saving grace was the snub nosed revolver. It was chambered for .357, and it had a holster that looked like it was designed to be strapped to an ankle. While I wasn't ready to go putting guns on my limbs, it wasn't a bad fall back gun even if it did only carry five rounds.

"That's the third time you've checked the guns," Amy said from behind me. "We're good, Dave. The guns are cleaned, all the magazines are loaded, our swords are cleaned, sharp and oiled, and our vests are almost dry. Your boots are the only things that still need to dry, and that's because you won't take them off." She stepped up beside me and nudged me with her shoulder.

"Sorry," I told her. "I'm a worrier when I don't have a clear plan."

"What, 'find an encrypted radio' isn't a plan?" she asked.

"It isn't what you'd call a plan so much as a guideline; a goal, really," I said in a bad pirate accent.

"You must really be stressed," she said, laughter in her voice. "You went five whole minutes without a movie quote. You chill. I'll keep an eye on things."

"Okay. I'll just make sure the rest of the gear is okay-" I started to say.

"Five times," Amy cut me off. "Seriously, you've already poked and prodded at it five times. We have a week's worth of food, all the other gear is fine. The only thing you haven't checked out is the sleeping bag. Why don't you give it a test run and let me know if it's working okay." I held up my hands and sat down on the tailgate to take my boots off. As soon as the first one came off, she took it from me and set it near the fire base for the Kelley Kettle. The second one ended up on the other side a moment later.

"Wake me up in… three hours," I said, yawning partway through the sentence.

"Whatever you say," she said as she headed for the ladder that led into the barn's upper level. While I wasn't happy about how flippant she sounded, I figured I could trust her to wake me up if she got too tired. I crawled into the bed of the truck and took a look into the cab. The keys were still in the ignition, just like they had been an hour ago. Through the front windshield, I could see the truck's shadow against the doors, cast by the faint light of the fire behind the tailgate. Behind my seat, the box of radio parts I'd grabbed from Radio Shack while Amy was updating her wardrobe was still secure. Satisfied for the moment that we were okay, I lowered myself onto the sleeping bag.

I woke to the sound of my own voice in my ears and a vague memory of a zombified Maya trying to tear my throat out with her teeth. My heart was pounding in my chest as my head came off the pillow. It was dark, and I was okay. Beside me, I heard the soft rasp of a girl's snore, then a hand fell on my shoulder.

"'Sokay, Dave," Amy muttered sleepily. "You're awright…jus' a badream." She patted my shoulder a couple of times before her hand fell away. I sat upright a second later.

"Amy!" I snapped. "What the hell are you doing? Wake the hell up!" I heard the rustle of fabric and a moment later blue light flooded the bed of the truck. I squinted and snatched the LED flashlight from Amy's hand and pointed it in her direction. She propped herself up on her elbows and squinted at me.

"Damn it Dave," she groaned at me. "Chill out. We're fine."

"We're not fine! You were supposed to wake me up so I could take the next watch. What if someone attacked us?"

"The coyotes would warn us before they got close," she said as she let herself fall back onto her sleeping bag. I stopped dead at that.

"Coyotes?" I asked. She nodded and pointed toward the outside of the truck as I heard a short bark nearby. Another bark answered it, then a third gave a longer bark with a high pitched yowl at the end.

"Yeah, they showed up about an hour after you fell asleep," she said through a yawn. "Go take a look." Determined to do just that, I turned the light to the tailgate and found my boots near the end of my sleeping bag. I stuck my feet in them and did a sloppy job of tying them without lacing them all the way up, then climbed the ladder and headed for the opening at the front of the barn. The quarter moon was low on the horizon, and in its faint light, I could see three coyotes sitting on their haunches and looking up at me. One of them yipped at me twice, then gave out another longer bark. In the distance, I heard a coyote howl, and the three outside answered. Then silence fell again, and the one that had barked at me looked back up at me for a moment before it trotted around to one side of the barn. I shrugged and let out a grunt before I retreated back to the truck.

I wasn't sure how long I laid there and tried to get back to sleep, but it felt like it was forever. Eventually, I crawled out of the truck and grabbed the AR, then made my way back to the loft. The moon had set by the time I settled back into place, so I concentrated on listening as I let my eyes adjust to the dark. Without the usual light pollution obscuring it, the Milky Way was a ribbon of stardust overhead, and I spent most of the next few hours alternating between marveling at the sky and listening for anything approaching. Eventually, the stars faded and the gray light of dawn crept across the sky behind me.

By the time Amy woke up, I had water boiling and breakfast was about to be rehydrated. Freeze-dried food was still the best thing I knew how to put together without an ice chest and a full camp stove. Amy slid out of the truck bed feet first and slipped her shoes on before she came over and sat down. Before, she'd never been a morning person, but she was clear eyed and alert as she took the bowl I handed her.

After breakfast, I started Amy's driving lessons by letting her drive the truck out of the barn and a little ways down the dirt road to get her used to it. Half an hour later, we were back on the road, with the barn cleaned up behind us and our gear stowed. It felt good to have my vest back on and the Deuce close to hand. We headed north, further into Nebraska for a little while, then turned west on another farm road. After a few miles, Amy pointed ahead. I followed the line of her finger to a white building on the right side of the road. "We're alive! 4 miles N" had been painted in red on the side of it with an arrow pointing in the right direction.

"You think we should check it out?" Amy asked.

"They might be able to tell us if there's an armory nearby or something. Might be worth checking out."

I looked over to her, and she shrugged. People were always a crap shoot. But, you also never won if you never took the chance. I took the turn just past the white building, and shook my head at the red "Infected inside. Do not enter" stenciled in red paint on the door. About three miles down the road, I pulled over and turned the truck off.

"I'm going to go on ahead and check things out. If things look okay, I'll call you in. But if you don't hear from me in about thirty minutes, give one call out. If I don't answer, or if I say 'All is well', go back to the last intersection we passed before we turned and wait until tomorrow morning. If I don't make it back to you then, head for Wyoming." I watched her face to see if she was going to argue with me, but she just gave me a dark look and nodded. Not terribly reassured, I tuned the shortwave on the dash to the same frequency as the Marine radio I had and got out. I didn't want to risk losing the AR, so I grabbed the Mossberg and shrugged the Takedown's carrying case on my shoulders. I'd stocked it with some basic gear as well, so it would be a compact survival kit if I needed one. Geared up, I started walking.

At first, the only sound I could hear was my boots on the cracked asphalt. Then the sound of birds, insects and wind. But one thing was missing, a sound I'd even heard sometimes out in the forest with my grandfather as a kid: the soft hum of traffic. Even out here, the sound of a car would travel for a long way, and you could usually hear the sound of rubber on asphalt. I walked for about twenty minutes, and finally found signs of human habitation. Oddly enough, it was the barnyard smell that hit me first. Then, I caught the scent of wood smoke on the wind as the road ahead of me curved around a hill that rose up on my right. As I rounded the curve, several bodies came into view. All of them were lying sprawled on the road as if they'd been left where they fell. I brought the shotgun up and sidestepped to my left, scanning left and right with the shotgun. On the far side of the road from me was a chest high stone wall that led to a metal gate blocking a road that ran up the hill and curved out of sight to the left. I didn't see anyone pointing a gun at me, but that didn't mean someone wasn't there. Slowly, I approached one of the bodies and spared a glance down at it. Dessicated brain matter was pooled around the back of its head, and its eyes were milky white, but I could still see the black veins running through them, a sure sign the corpse had been infected before it died. Without turning away from the gate, I checked the other corpses. All of them had bullet holes through their heads, and all of them looked infected. Whoever had been doing the shooting didn't seem to be targeting the living. I didn't see any bloodstains, so I figured they hadn't shot any living people and hid the bodies. Still, I didn't feel like taking chances.

With my shoulder blades twitching, I stalked up to the gate and looked it over to see how it was secured. A chain was padlocked around one side, and a wire as tied to the chain itself. I followed the thin wire with my eyes as far as I could but it disappeared into the brush a few yards away from the fence. The wire itself was under a little tension, so I suspected it was weighted to prevent someone from simply cutting it to bypass it. Anything that ran into the gate would probably sound some kind of alarm, but little things like birds or the wind didn't seem likely to.

Since I didn't want to risk drawing any infected, I figured the best thing to do was to ring the doorbell. Before I could chicken out, I reached out and grabbed the top of the gate and moved it back and forth a few times, then darted to the left side, toward the gate's hinges, and knelt down beside the wall where I wouldn't be immediately visible to someone coming down the path.

A few minutes later, I heard the slow, measured sound of cautious footsteps approaching. A man in blue jeans and a gray button down work shirt came into view, his scuffed and worn work boots making only the faintest of sounds as he crept up on the gate. Most of his face was obscured by the stock of the rifle he held against his shoulder and a John Deere ballcap. Weathered hands were wrapped around the rifle's stock and fore end, and I could see the corded lines of muscle under her skin as he slowly lowered the gun. The gun's receiver looked familiar, and I guessed he was carrying one of the original versions of the M14, the rifle the M39 I'd lost in Kansas City was based on.

"Howdy," I said as he straightened. The gun came up and pointed in my direction. The man's eyes were wide in his narrow face, but he didn't pull the trigger.

"Stand up where I can see you," he barked. I got to my feet slowly and grabbed the shotgun by the barrel with my right hand. As I straightened, I held it out away from me with the stock in the air.

"If I had meant to shoot you, I would have done it before I said hello," I said as I stepped away from the wall. "I just figured you were a pretty good shot from a distance, so I didn't want you to think I was infected or anything. I'd hate to get shot by mistake."

"You damn near did anyway," he said as he lowered the rifle again. "Who are you?"

"My name's Dave. I'm a survivor, just like you. I saw your sign down by the road. Figured I'd come by, see if I could help out, or maybe trade a bit. What's your name?"

"Del," the man answered cautiously. "I didn't put up no sign. Nearest road's about five miles from here." His eyes narrowed, and I could almost hear the alarm bells going off in his head.

"It looked pretty old, and it said ten miles down. Look, Del, I'm not asking you to take us in or anything. Hell, you don't even have to let us in the gate. We're not looking to stay in the area. I'm just looking for some information, and I'm willing to trade for it."

"Us? Who's with you?" he demanded, his eyes scanning the road and the brush behind me.

"My daughter. She's parked down the road a little ways." I didn't like the way his eyes shifted or the speculative look he got on his face. Then he turned his head to look back up the road he'd come down, and I heard a woman's voice.

"Del, you all right?" the woman asked. She walked into view a second later, a thin woman with plain brown hair and dark circles under her eyes. Her floral print shirt clung to her spare frame, and her denim skirt covered her narrow legs to mid-calf, where a pair of cowboy boots took over..

"I'm fine, Penny," he answered.

"Who're you talking to honey?" she asked when she caught sight of me.

"His name's Dave," he said. "Him and his daughter are just passin' through, and he was looking to trade for some information."

"Hi, ma'am," I said as I slung the shotgun and waved with my left hand. They exchanged a look, and she nodded.

"Why don't you have your daughter come on up, and we'll see if we can help each other out," Del said. His wife smiled at me as I stepped back and pulled the radio from its pocket on my vest.

"Amy, it's Dave. You got your ears on?" I said.

"Sorry, left them in my other purse," Amy replied a few seconds later.

"Smart ass," I said. "We're mostly good here. Come on up."

"Mostly?" she asked.

"Yeah, mostly," I said as I turned away from Del and Penny. "But an ace up your sleeve wouldn't be taken amiss." I pitched the last part low enough that it wouldn't carry more than a couple of feet.

"Roger that," Amy said. "I'll be right there." I turned to face Del and Penny to find that Del was opening the gate.

"Why don't y'all come up and have a bite to eat with us," Penny said.

"We wouldn't want to impose," I said. "I know times are…well, strange, and every little bite of food helps."

"Nonsense," Penny said with a smile and a wave of her hand. "We've got it to spare, and it's been more than a week since we've seen anyone out here. All we can get on the radio is that awful government station and the Solomon Bible University Gospel Hour out of Tulsa."

"You still have power?" I asked as I heard the truck coming up the road.

29

"For a few hours a day," Del said as he swung the gate out and gestured for Amy to drive on in. She stopped at the edge of the road and looked to me.

"Sorry, she's just learning to drive," I said. "Hop in, we'll give you a lift the rest of the way." Del had Penny climb in the back with Amy, and took the passenger seat to guide me the rest of the way up the hill. The road forked two times on the way up, and Del informed me that the first fork led down to the gardens his grandfather had carved into the side of the hill, and the second went to the barn and animal pens at the base of the hill. Then we hit the top of the hill, and I let the truck roll to a stop and just stared in awe at the view. A two story house dominated the plateau before me, with a thick stand of trees on the north side. To the south, we could see for a couple of miles. Rolling fields were edged with lines of trees and narrow gray roads, a postcard perfect tableau. Trees blocked the view to the west, but to the east, the only thing between us and the horizon was a windmill and a waist high metal tank that was filled with water.

A boy about Amy's age was standing on the front porch with a double barreled shotgun in his hands, looking us over with a frown on his face. Off to the south side of the house, I could see a dog on a chain that was connected to a tree. A circle of dirt marked his territory, and he sat looking at us from the edge of his domain. When we got out of the truck, his tail thumped in the dirt behind him a few times, then went still. Del came around the truck and gestured for the boy to come over.

"This is Tad, he's my oldest," he said as the boy approached. Tad was a wider version of his father, with plenty of baby fat still rounding out his cheeks and a sullen, almost drowsy look about him. He stuck out a hand and clamped onto mine with an almost painful grip. "Tad, this is Dave."

"Pleased to meet you," he said with a smile that didn't make me think he was.

"That's quite a grip you have," I said as I extricated my hand from his clutches. His hand wasn't soft, but hard work wasn't something he seemed to be as familiar with as his father.

"He's gonna grow up to be stronger than his dad," Del said with a smile.

"You said he was your oldest?" I said.

"His brother and sister are at their lessons," Penny offered as she and Amy came up. "They struggle with math and English, especially his sister. But, what can you expect of a girl?" Her laugh was a staccato sound, almost a nervous reaction to her own attempt at humor. "But, she needs to master the basics to help run the farm."

"I hope we'll get to meet them later," I said. "This is my daughter Amy," I said as she stepped up beside me.

"Hi," Tad said as he stepped up close to her and held his hand out. "I'm Tad."

"I heard," she said as she took his hand to shake it. Instead, he pulled it up to his face and did a clumsy job of kissing the back of her hand.

"You can take your guns off," Del said with a smile. "There's no zombies left out this way, unless some wander in from the road. Tad killed about thirty of 'em, and I did for the rest. Besides, guns in the house make the little lady nervous." He laughed, and Penny ducked her head with a smile.

"Sure, Del," I said, letting my Missouri accent creep a little further into my voice. "We'll just toss them in the truck." Amy followed me to the rear of the truck, wiping the back of her hand against her pant leg as she went. I opened the back up and undid my assault vest.

"Are you sure about this?" she said softly as I unbuckled the gun belt.

"Not exactly," I admitted. "But I'm not hearing banjo music."

"Me, either," she said as she undid the holster on her hip. "I'm getting more of the creepy stalker vibe. Especially off of Don Juan over there." I chuckled at the barb and eyed the black utility vest I'd lifted from the deputy's cruiser, wishing I could find an excuse to put it on.

"You and me both," I said. "Rule eight and rule twelve definitely apply here."

"I'm thinking all of them from four through nine are in play," she said as she slipped her little .22 revolver into the cargo pocket on her right leg. I tucked the holster for the revolver into my waist band and pulled my shirt out to cover it.

"How many guns have you got?" Tad asked as he came along the side of the truck.

31

"A couple each," I said as his eyes went wide at the array of firearms. "Most of it is side arms, though." We slid our gear into the bed of the truck and closed the tailgate and the camper shell up. Both of us still had at least two knives visible, but I also knew Amy had a ZT Spike hidden away on her somewhere. Again, I felt that naked sensation of being unarmed and every step away from the truck and my sword made my palms itch. Tad escorted us inside and set his shotgun in a rack on the wall beside the front door. He led us to the front room and invited us to have a seat. A couch and a love seat made an L on one side of the room, while two recliners sat on either side of a table with a lamp that stuck up from the back of it. A pair of bookshelves sat on either side of the doorway we came in through, and a dormant television sat under one of the windows. A broad fireplace took up the far wall, and thick rugs covered the hardwood floor in the open space between the seating arrangements. The TV, once the center of the room, was now on the outskirts.

"Polly!" Del bellowed. "Get down here and help your mother with lunch!" As the sound of footsteps came closer, Penny stepped into the room with a pitcher of tea and some glasses on a tray.

"Would you like some tea while you wait?" she asked. "I'm sorry there's no ice, we just use it to for storage." She poured a glass and handed it to Tad, who took it and sat down on the love seat without a word. Then she offered Amy and me a glass. Maya would have been proud of her girl as she smiled and offered the woman a sweet "Thank you!" I followed her example with a little more reserve.

Tad patted the love seat beside him and said "Take a load off your feet," his gaze on Amy. She nodded to him and sat on the couch. For a moment, I considered sitting next to Tad to mess with him, but instead I sat next to Amy and took a sip of my tea. It was a little bitter with just a hint of honey to it.

"So, how many zombies have *you* killed?" Tad asked me as his father walked into the room with a glass of tea in his hand. "I've killed thirty three." I hesitated, debating on whether I should play the game or let him have his pride. Not wanting to wound his ego, I shook my head.

"I haven't really been counting," I said, which was partly true. I hadn't been in a position to keep track of zombie kills, usually because most times that I ended up fighting them recently, it had been against nearly overwhelming numbers of the damn things.

"So far, the best guess is about three hundred and fifty," Amy said. I did a double take and felt like my jaw was sliding halfway down my chest.

"Total?" I asked without thinking. She nodded with a smug grin on her face.

"Yep," she said. "Guns and sword. And that was before the night we left KC."

"Who the hell was keeping track of *that*?"

"Everyone," she said. "Willie had a hundred and eighty, Kent was right behind him with one-seventy-five."

"You were in Kansas City?" Del asked.

"No way," Tad said. "The radio said Kansas City burned to the ground." His tone was challenging, and he looked more than a little put out.

"It was on fire, but it hadn't burnt to the ground, at least not as of a couple of days ago." I gave them a very abridged version of our trip so far, leaving out my brushes with Keyes and the DHS, and glossing over the details of our run in and escape from the Disciples of the Anointed. By the time I was done, even Tad had lost a little of the dejected look on his face. Del had shown a lot more interest in the story, and had asked a few questions that I'd had to dodge as I went along.

"Lunch is done," Penny said from the doorway to the dining room as I told him about the road out of the city. We followed Del and Tad in to find five place settings at the table and several covered dishes.

"Are we going to get to meet your other two kids?" she asked. Penny shook her head and let out a long suffering sigh.

"I'm afraid not today," she said. "They haven't been behaving very well since things…changed. Tad handled it much better, but Polly and Will are just so difficult. They're having lunch in their rooms."

"I'll go up and handle things a little later on," Del said somberly, and Penny nodded. "But let's go ahead and eat first." I

33

tried to keep my face neutral as we sat down and Del asked his son to say grace. Not seeing the other two kids just added to the creepy feeling that had settled at the base of my neck, but it wasn't enough to really do anything with. Tad recited a short blessing over the meal, and all our heads came up after he said "Amen." The dishes were uncovered to reveal chicken, mashed potatoes and corn, with a loaf of brown bread and a crockery bowl with butter in it. It certainly seemed like there was plenty to go around, and we dug in. Penny's cooking was a welcome change to my half-assed campfire culinary skill, and while it was a little plain, it was, like most meals I'd eaten in the last two weeks, delicious in a way very little had been since I'd come back from Iraq.

"Dave and Amy just came from Kansas City," Del offered from the head of the table as the initial onslaught of the food died down. "Seems the roads south of here are pretty clear, except for some raiders down near Topeka." Across from me, Penny's face became a little more animated.

"Maybe we can go check on your brother's place," she said. Del's expression clouded a little at that, but he nodded.

"I also want to head down to the seed co-op and see if I can find some wheat and corn to plant for next year. This year's sorghum crop'll see us through the winter, but I'm going to get mighty tired of the taste of it by spring."

"I was wondering if you knew of any National Guard units in the area," I asked.

"Well, there's the big base out in Omaha, but I don't think anyone would want to go there," Del said after a moment's thought. "Our neighbor used to report to Lincoln, but that's another big city, and even the government says to leave them alone."

"What about that place west of here?" Penny asked. "Remember, my brother used to go there for a couple of weeks every summer."

"Hastings," Del supplied. "And I think there's a unit out of Grand Island, too." Conversation turned to small talk after that. In the post zombie world that included where zombies were likely to be found and how winter might affect them. Amy and I took turns explaining about the different kinds of ghouls we'd encountered in Kansas City, though we left out the less appetite killing details as I dolloped out some of the sorghum molasses and mixed it with butter to sop up with my bread. Amy followed my example with a doubtful look on her face until she took her first bite. After that, she didn't utter a word until her plate was clean.

"Dave, you mentioned doing some trading," Del said as he leaned back in his chair. "Why don't you and I do some bargaining." Everyone got up from the table, and I grabbed my plate to take it into the kitchen.

"Don't worry about that," Penny said as she took the plate from me. "I'll take care of it. You fellows go talk business." As I relinquished my hold on the plate, I half heard Tad asking Amy if she'd like to see his motorbike. I turned her way in time to see her shrug and agree. Del led me back through the front room and out onto the porch.

"So, what do you two need?" he asked me as we stood watching the two teens walk toward a path in the trees to the north.

"Aside from cooking lessons from your wife, the first thing I'd like to get is some gas if you have any to spare," I said. "Fresh food is always welcome, and I wouldn't mind some of that sorghum molasses, either. I have about a hundred and twenty rounds for that M14 of yours in six magazines, and we could spare a few rounds of twelve gauge for that double barrel scattergun your boy was carrying."

We settled down for some serious haggling at the tailgate of the truck, and I ended up throwing in one of the two bottles of Johnny Walker Black Label I'd picked up on the way out of KC. Amy and Tad walked up as we were nailing down the specifics.

"Dad gave me the shotgun when we first heard about the problems in Omaha," Tad was saying as they came closer. "I've been protecting the farm since the first zombies showed up." He tried to make it sound casual, like shooting zombies was no big thing.

"Dave gave me his Ruger when we crashed in Kansas City," Amy said as she pulled her vest toward her. "And he gave me this while we were trying to get out of the hospital." She pulled the nine millimeter Browning out of her vest and dropped the magazine into her other hand, then pulled the slide back and locked it into place before turning it over in her hand and handing it to Tad butt first. The whole process had taken less than five seconds, and she'd handled the pistol like a pro. Tad's brows crowded together over his nose as he took the gun from her.

"Aren't you afraid this is a little too much gun for you?" he asked as he looked it over. He missed the warning she gave him with the irritated Spock brow lift. "I mean, a twenty two is fine for a girl, but anything bigger than that..." he let the sentence trail off as she took the gun from him and let the slide pop forward before she slammed the magazine into the butt. She grabbed her vest and stalked off, leveling a cold glare at Tad.

"What's her problem?" he asked as he joined his father on the porch.

"She prefers to be treated like an equal," I said calmly. Father and son laughed for a moment, and I bit my tongue as Penny brought out the boxes with the vegetables and three jars of molasses. Tad followed us over to the garage, and helped Del pump five gallons of gas into the jerry can I'd taken from the truck. Once I had that loaded, I looked up at the sky as if to gauge how much daylight I had left, then went to the cab of the truck and pulled out my cache tube. I retrieved five of the ten silver ounces I had stashed in it and tucked them into my pocket, then whistled to get Amy's attention.

"Get me out of here before I put a bullet in Captain Chauvinist," she muttered under her breath when she trotted up.

"Just one more piece of business," I said softly. "Unless you don't want me to trade for any books." She bit her lower lip and took a sharp breath, then grimaced and nodded.

"They do have those two bookshelves," she said. We turned and headed back for the porch.

"So, Del, I was wondering," I said as we climbed the steps, "would you be willing to trade a few books?"

"If I thought I could get away with a second bottle of whiskey in the house, I'd trade you a whole shelf full of 'em," he said with a laugh. "But the wife won't have it. If you've got something else to trade, though, I wouldn't mind letting some go." By way of answer, I reached into my pocket and pulled out two of the round coins.

"Well, I have a little silver," I said as I opened my hand.

"What's that other one?" Tad demanded. I looked down and bit off a curse. Instead of two silver rounds, I'd pulled out the Special Forces challenge coin Captain Adams had given me along with one of the one ounce coins. I slipped it back into my pocket and pulled out another silver round.

"It's a challenge coin," I said. "Got it from some soldiers I helped out back in Springfield." Tad seemed like he was still oblivious, but Del's eyes were on me with a little more intensity than I would have liked. "So, you interested in a trade?"

"Sure," he said slowly. "Say, two books for one of those silver coins?"

"Make it three and you have a deal," I countered.

"Three paperbacks. A hardback book counts as two." I pretended to think it over then nodded like I wasn't exactly happy about it. He led us inside and gestured toward the two bookshelves. Pretty much every Louis L'Amour book I could think of was on the shelf at eye level, plus a long line of Zane Grey novels shared space with copies of the Farmer's Almanac on the shelf below that. The bottom shelf held a few surprises, some old school science fiction and fantasy and one thick Reader's Digest Condensed Book from 1974. I grabbed the Reader's Digest book, a Conan title and a novel by H Beam Piper called The Fuzzy Files. Amy came over to me with a forced smile on her face and held out four books for consideration while I handed her my picks. She'd gone for the classics with To Kill A Mockingbird and Treasure Island mixed in with Sherlock Holmes and Little Women. I looked over at her with a frown. Of the four titles she had handed me, only Sherlock Holmes would have had any interest for her, since she would have imagined Holmes looking like Benedict Cumberbatch. She shrugged at my look, then waved toward the shelf.

"I wasn't sure what was good," she said with a pained look on her face. "Could you look and make a few suggestions for me when I get back?" I nodded and headed for the shelf on the right of the door as she asked Del where the bathroom was. She made her way out of the front room and I set the four books on the top shelf, then started looking over the books. My eyes roamed across the titles, then stopped at the end of the row on the top shelf. Tucked in beside an old Bible was a title I had only heard horror stories about, one I'd hoped never to see: The Obedient Child, by David Bethlehem. Bethlehem's methods were harsh, and more than one child abuse case had come from people using them. If I knew Amy, she wasn't in the bathroom, she was snooping, looking for confirmation of what she suspected was going on. As one part of my brain speculated on what might happen, I pulled two of the books Amy had handed me off the stack and set them aside. My attention was only half on the books in front of me, though I managed to find one other book I thought Amy would like.

The sound of a blow came to my ears, but it was Amy's voice that cried out in pain, and Penny who started yelling. I ran for the stairs as another blow sounded, and someone fell to the floor. When I reached the top of the stairs, I found Penny scrambling to her feet with Amy a few feet down the darkened hall from her. A three foot length of plumbing tube dangled from Penny's right hand, and she brought her arm back as she got to her feet.

"Brat!" she screeched as she started to swing. Amy stepped forward as she brought her left arm up to take the blow and Penny doubled over with a violent gasp. She went to straighten again, and when her arm came back again, I grabbed her by the wrist.

"Don't touch her again," I growled as I spun her to face me.

"Someone needs to break that little bitch's will," the woman hissed at me. "And if you're not man enough to do it, God help me I *will*!" The sound of boots on the stairs came from down the hall, and Penny backed away from me with a cruel smile on her face. Del and Tad emerged behind her and she ducked past them to glare at me from over her son's shoulder.

"You okay?" I asked Amy as the tableau held.

"Yeah, I'm fine," she said, her voice trembling from anger. "You saw the book?" I nodded. "It's about like that."

"You saw it?"

"She's lying!" Penny snapped before Amy could answer. "She didn't see anything!"

"Then you won't mind if I see for myself," I said and turned toward the door on my right. From the corner of my eye, I saw Penny and Tad start to smile, but their expressions turned to horrified gasps as I lifted my foot and drove my heel into the door beside the knob. Wood splintered as the door swung away from me. The room was dark, with the window covered with a piece of thick, black fabric. I nodded to Amy and she stepped into the room to pull the curtain aside. The wash of light revealed a girl handcuffed to an eyebolt that had been set into the floor in the far corner of the room. She looked like she couldn't have weighed eighty pounds soaking wet, with wide, dark eyes that darted from Amy to me and back. Her dark hair hung in lanky strands, and the smell of stale urine hit my nose. The shapeless dress that clung to her shoulders was stained and ripped, with bruised flesh revealed by each tear. My fists clenched as I turned toward Del and Penny but the hallway was empty.

"I'll get her loose," Amy said. Her left hand was already in her front pocket, and I went to the next door down. It opened after a couple of kicks, and I found myself faced with a boy clad in jean shorts who couldn't have been more than nine chained in the corner of that room. He stared at me silently as I walked toward him and went to work on the handcuff around his left wrist.

"Hi, I'm Dave," I said as the handcuff opened. "What's your name?" He just looked at me for a moment, then drew back as far away as he could. I rocked back on my heels and watched him cower and tremble. What the hell had I been thinking? That he was just going to rush to the arms of someone who kicked the door in? I nodded and rose slowly, then turned away as I tucked the handcuffs in my back pocket, hoping against reality that he'd understand I wasn't going to hurt him. Amy was waiting for me at the door with his sister's hand in hers. Polly inched away from me, and I stepped to the side.

"Is he okay?" she asked.

"He's scared of me," I said. "He might trust you." Polly pulled free of Amy's hand and rushed to the boy's side. They clung to each other and watched us with wide eyes. I pulled the door shut and turned to her.

"We can't fix this, Amy," I said. "I don't know how, and we don't have the resources."

"We can't just turn our backs, either!" she said.

"You're right, we can't. And we won't."

"We'll figure something out," she said. "After we deal with the Manson family."

"They're going to be waiting for us," I said. She nodded and pulled her pistol from the cargo pocket on her right leg. No one was waiting at the bottom of the steps, but a glance toward the rack by the door showed the shotgun and the M14 absent from it. I pulled the revolver from the holster and pointed toward the back door. Amy nodded and padded silently to the rear of the house, while I went to the front window. Father and son were standing between the porch and the truck, guns in hand. Penny stood behind and between them, her lips pressed together in a sharp line. Once again, I wished I'd worn my vest. Without it, I only had wit and luck to count on, and neither one would stop a bullet. I went back into the front room and grabbed the offending book.

"I'm coming out," I said as I let the door open an inch or two. Slowly, I pushed the door open the rest of the way and watched to see what they'd do. Del brought his rifle up and aimed it at the door while Tad pointed his shotgun at it without bothering to aim.

"You get the hell away from my kids, mister," Del said. "I want you off my property now!"

"Near as I can tell, the biggest danger to your kids is you," I said as I stepped out onto the porch.

"You have no right to tell us how to raise our kids," Penny said from behind her husband.

"I was talking about your husband and your son pointing guns at me without knowing where your other two kids are," I said as I turned and moved to my right. Their guns and their eyes followed me. "Now, I'd love to be as far away from you folks as I could get right now, but you're standing between me and my truck."

"I think we're standing between you and *my* new truck," Tad said. Amy darted from the side of the house as he brought his shotgun up a little higher for emphasis. I paused and looked at him for a moment. I still needed time for Amy to get the drop on them, but Tad was just as impulsive as she was. If anyone was going to start shooting, it was him.

"Son," Del said slowly.

"I want that truck Dad," Tad said emphatically. "Think of all the stuff in it." Del nodded after a moment, and Tad smiled.

"Right now, kid," I said slowly as I saw Amy pull the camper's rear hatch open, "I'd be thinking *real* hard about the Golden Rule." The comment had the desired effect, as father and son exchanged glances.

"You get your daughter and you get the hell off our land," Penny snapped after a few seconds. "If you know what's good for you," she added with a smirk.

"Hell, you ought to be grateful we don't just shoot you now," Tad said. All three of them froze in place when Amy racked a round into the Mossberg.

"Funny," she said, her voice tight. "I was just about to say the same thing to you assholes." All eyes went to her, and I brought the revolver up. As I sighted on Del's back, I wondered if I was going to survive Maya's reaction when she saw what two weeks with me had done to her little girl.

"Drop the guns," I said as I pulled the hammer back. It wasn't necessary, but it got the point across. "Now." Tad almost threw the shotgun down, while Del took the M14 by the barrel and laid it down on the ground in front of him. "Turn around and put your hands against the truck." All three of them glared at me, but they did it. I stepped down off the porch and picked up the shotgun and broke it open. Once I'd extracted the two shells, I dropped it and picked up the rifle. Amy came around to my side as I dropped the magazine and pulled the charging handle to clear the round from the chamber. With their weapons empty, I pulled the handcuffs from my pocket and threw them on the ground between Dell and Tad.

"Cuff yourself to him, right hand to right hand." Amy handed me the other set of cuffs, and I tossed them next to Penny. "You do the same, left hand to left hand with your husband."

"You better think real hard about what you do to us," Del said. "Because once I get loose, you're gonna regret it." Beside him, Tad was red faced and shaking, whether from fear or anger

I couldn't tell. I pretended to think for a moment before I answered.

"I recall someone thinking I should be grateful that they didn't just shoot me," I said. "So I was thinking about that." Tad let out a moan.

"I wasn't part of any of that, I swear!" he blubbered. "They made me go along with it!"

"Relax, kid, I'm not gonna shoot you. But I meant what I said about the Golden Rule. See, I have some rules of my own. Rule Twenty Three goes something like this: Don't walk away if someone needs help. So, what am I going to do with you? I'm still not sure. But I think I know where to look for some ideas," I said as I held up the book.

Chapter 3
Karma

~ At his best, man is the noblest of animals; separated from law and justice, he is the worst. ~
Aristotle

"You can't do this to me!" Penny screamed from the other side of the basement door. I sighed as I closed it and made my way through the kitchen, picking up two bowls of oatmeal as I went. In the dining room, three children now sat at the table, each one studiously not looking at anything but the bowl in front of them. I went past as quietly as I could, but halfway down the hallway I heard the clinking of silverware on plates stop. Amy's voice came from the dining room, soft and reassuring. The sound of eating still didn't resume until I was halfway up the stairs. The door to the little boy's room opened easily under my hand, and Del looked up at me from the same spot his younger son had been chained yesterday afternoon. Like his son, he only wore a pair of jeans. The red marks from the beatings I had given him stood out on his back and shoulders, and he shivered from the cold. I set the bowl down at the edge of his reach and stepped back.

"What do you have to say for yourself?" I asked as he reached for it.

"You got no right to do this to me, and if I get loose, I'm gonna beat the shit outta you," he growled. I nudged the bowl out of his reach with my foot.

"For treating you like you treat your own children," I said. He glared at me. "Everything you told me I couldn't do to you, you did to them. The way I see it, this right here, the last eighteen hours or so...*that's* what you have a right to for the rest of your life." I nudged the bowl back toward him.

"No one tells me how to raise my kids," he said around the first spoonful of plain oatmeal. I turned and walked to the door.

"You let Bethlehem's book do that for you already," I said from the doorway. "Funny how his methods are okay to use on your kids, but it pisses you off when I use them on you." I pulled the door shut and went to the next one. Tad was curled up in a sniffling ball in the corner. His head came up when the door

43

opened. I set the bowl down in easy reach of him and stepped back. Unlike his parents, he'd been spared the beatings, the dousing with water and had been fed at the same time as the other kids.

"What do you have to say for yourself?" I repeated.

"I didn't do anything," he said as he grabbed the bowl. "It was all Mom and Dad, they locked my brother and sisters up. There wasn't anything I could do about it." I shook my head at the litany. He'd turned on his parents before we even got them into the house, and told us about Lena, his older half-sister who had been locked in the basement since she was a little girl. An embarrassment to her mother because she was born out of wedlock, she'd been hidden away all her life. If he'd been hoping for some mercy from me by betraying his parents though, he'd been disappointed.

"You didn't do anything," I said. He nodded quickly, looking up at me with a hopeful smile. "That's your crime. You let your brother and your sisters suffer while you enjoyed a normal life." His face fell at that, but I was pretty sure he wasn't disappointed in himself. Still, if there was hope for any of them, it was with him. I took a deep breath, then pulled the key to his handcuffs from my pocket. "Finish your food, then go and unlock your parents. Meet us out front." I walked out and went down the steps. Amy waited for me with a bowl of the same stew the other kids had been eating.

"No thanks," I said. "I don't have much of an appetite right now." She nodded.

"Me, either," she said as she turned and took it into the dining room. The other three kids were sitting in the front room, huddled on the couch and looking worried. I walked past them and out to the front porch. The morning sun was casting long shadows across the fields, and mist was rising in long, narrow patches from the ground. It should have been beautiful. Amy led the three kids out onto the porch, and for a moment, I got to see them smile like normal kids. Then the front door opened and Del walked across the porch, his head down. Penny followed him, and as soon as she saw the girls, she moved toward them.

"You worthless little-" was all she got out before I punched her. She staggered back and fell off the porch.

"You will never lay a hand on those kids again," I said. She got up and stared daggers at me.

"You won't always be around, you self-righteous son of a bitch," Del said. I came off the porch and shoved him against the side of the truck with my forearm across his neck.

"But I will be back," I said as he struggled. "And if either of you so much as touches one of these children in anger, I swear to you. I. Will. Bury. You." His face went pale at that, and he stopped fighting against me. I stepped back and let him fall to the ground, then turned to Tad, who had been the last one out. He was ashen faced and stood stock still.

"You," I said sternly. His eyes locked on me. "You didn't do anything. That ends now. If they're not treated the same way you used to be, you speak up. You do everything you can to stop it. Do you understand?" He nodded quickly. Finally I turned back to Del.

"You have one week, maybe two before I come check on you," I said, my voice trembling as I fought to keep from hitting him again. "If these children aren't all alive, healthy and on the mend when I come back, I'm going to chain the two of you to the floor in one of those rooms and leave you there to die. Am I understood?" His eyes narrowed, but he nodded slowly. I stepped back, and felt a creeping sensation up the back of my neck. Amy stood, and I turned to look over my shoulder. She trotted to the edge of the hilltop and looked down, then turned back to me.

"Ghouls!" she called out. I ran to the truck and pulled the Deuce and Amy's sword belt from the cab. "You read my mind," she said as she buckled it on.

"I need to leave them with an example they won't forget," I sad as I drew my blade. "But I need you to stay out of this fight and keep an eye on the Manson family here." Her jaw clenched as she frowned at me. She nodded and stepped back a couple of paces with an expression on her face like she'd just eaten a raw lemon. I moved forward and looked down the hill at the trio of ghouls that were racing up the slope toward us. Two wore t-shirts and jeans, and one was clad in the remains of a waitress' outfit. The one in the lead was uttering a low growl as he came at me, and all too soon, he was coming over the edge of the hill. I

45

held the blade with both hands and stepped into the swing. The blade caught him just above the shoulder and sliced through the front of his torso with a snapping sound as it clove through bones. The ghoul went down, its feet whipping forward as it fell on its back from the force of the blow. The other two stopped as they crested the edge of the hill, and did something I hadn't seen any stage one infected do before.

They stared at me. Their milky eyes seemed to move back and forth, and their noses twitched as they seemed to test the air. Then, as if that wasn't enough weirdness for one moment, they turned and ran. I transferred the sword to my right hand and grabbed my .45 from its holster as I went to the edge of the hill. The first ghoul dropped with one shot, and the second fell after I put two rounds into it. I dispatched the one I'd first killed with a stroke from my blade across its skull, and finished the other two off with a pair of short chops to the back of the head before I wiped my blade clean on the shirt of one of them. When I crested the hill again, all six members of the family were gathered by the truck.

"Okay, how did you pull that off?" Amy asked as I walked up beside her.

"I wish I knew, but I don't think it was just me," I said while I wiped the blade clean on the lead ghoul's shirt. "They're running in packs, maybe they're smart enough to know when they're facing whatever we are."

"I've never seen the fast ones run from anyone before," Tad said as we approached. "How did y'all know they were coming?" He looked at me like he'd never seen me before, and I wondered if I'd grown a second head or something. Even Penny was keeping a safe distance from me.

"I don't know," I said. "We just...do. We're really good at killing zombies. Those three probably broke through a fence last night somewhere. You might want to see if you can fix that."

"Um...how many have you killed?" Tad asked Amy.

"Seventy two," she replied. His jaw dropped for a second, then his mouth closed almost as quickly. I tossed the Deuce into the truck and pulled the magazine for the M14 from my pocket.

"Take care of them," I told Del as I handed it to him. "I don't need to remind you what'll happen if you don't." He shook his head.

"I'm not an idiot. But you'd better pray I never get the drop on you again, because I'll kill you the second I see you."

"I'll make sure you don't," I said. I made the decision not to tell him I'd field stripped both of their guns. Del stepped back, leaving Penny to stare at me with hate in her eyes. Tad went back to the porch and hovered near his brother and younger sister while Amy and Lena spoke softly. They shared a brief hug, then Amy went to the truck and got in. I got in on my side and started the truck, then backed up and headed for the road down.

"Do you think we actually did any good?" I asked her once we cleared the gate.

"No," she said after a few moments. "Are we really coming back?" I nodded.

"If we don't, I'll find someone to come back in our place. No matter what, if we can find a place for those kids, we're not leaving them there." We drove in silence for another minute.

"Are you mad at me for pushing things?" she asked. "Should I have left things alone?"

"No," I said. "I'm not mad at you. Mad about the situation, mad that we couldn't take those kids with us, mad about a lot of things. But not at you."

"I thought I was doing the right thing," she said.

"Kobayashi Maru, ensign," I said softly. "There was no right solution."

"Well, if they put Lena back in that basement, they're going to be in for a surprise," she said with a smile. "I hid one of my Spikes and a handcuff key behind a brick in the basement. I told her where to find it when she hugged me."

"Good job. Now you're starting to think like me," I said. "You're mom's going to kill me. But seriously, you did more good than I did back there."

"I just about got us killed," she said. "How do you figure I did more good?"

"To those kids, I was the violent stranger who kicked their doors in," I told her. "They were more frightened of me than of

47

their parents. You…I needed you to be what I couldn't. The one they trusted."

"I wish they knew you like I do," she said. "They wouldn't be afraid of you. I just don't get why we can't take them with us."

"Same reason I didn't want you coming with me when I left KC. Keyes and the DHS or whoever he works for are still looking for me. For now, all we can do is pray that things don't go really bad before we make it back." We drove along in silence after that, and turned west at the intersection where we'd found the sign. I still wondered who had painted it, but like so many things I wondered about lately, I resigned myself to not knowing.

The road we were on turned from a numbered highway into a dirt road, so we turned north to stay on US 75. A couple of miles further up, we found a sign that showed Auburn was less than twenty miles away. The road was mostly empty until we hit a little café with a small group of infected in the parking lot. They ran out into the road when they heard us coming, but the truck made short work of the three ghouls that got in its way. Twenty minutes later, we were pulling into Auburn, a town that boasted a population of a little over three thousand. The streets were empty, a contrast to the bigger towns we'd been to. Smoke rose in thin strands from deeper in town, but most of the place seemed intact. I slowed down as we hit J street, and started looking at signs. A shopping center loomed on our right, but it only seemed have a dozen or so zombies wandering around in the parking lot.

"Dave, look," Amy pointed to my left. A small, gray building labeled itself as "The Farmer's Pantry – Bulk Foods." No cars were parked in front of it, but a Ford truck was parked just behind it. I pulled into the parking lot and drew the SOCOM. Amy got out as I screwed the suppressor onto the big pistol's barrel and got out. Nothing seemed to be moving, so I made my way to the door. A white rectangle was taped to the glass from the inside.

"If you're alive, come on in and take what you need. Gale and I don't have much use for it now. Try to leave a little for the next person if you can, but if you take the last of what's here, please take this note down. Don't worry, we're not inside."

The door opened easily, and I stepped inside. The SOCOM's tac light illuminated half empty shelves. Whoever had been here before me had evidently taken the note to heart, and had left at least half of everything. Five gallon buckets of bulk foods like beans, flour and rice were stacked along one wall, while sacks of corn and grains took up half of the adjacent wall. Spices and canned goods were on the shelves on my right, and a display of grinders was on the counter in front of me. A lot of what was there, we wouldn't be able to use on the road, but some of it would come in handy later. Following the example of the person before me, I took one of the two grinders and only some of what was left, partly out of respect for the owners, and partly because we didn't have a lot of room in the truck.

"Next stop, a gas station," I said as I climbed back into the truck.

"There's one just up the street," Amy said. True to her word, there was a Casey's a hundred yards up, next to a pharmacy and across the street from a vision clinic. The pharmacy was gutted, the front doors and windows shattered. The convenience store didn't look much better, but it was worth checking out.

"Inside, use your pistol. Cover the side you're on," I said when we got out of the truck. "If you see something, don't be shy. Let me know."

"How do you know this shit?" she asked as we walked up to the open doors. "I mean, no offense, but you were some kind of radio guy, right?"

"Nate told me a lot of it when I was writing Operation Terror and The Frankenstein Code. Of course, knowing about it and actually doing it are really different." She gave me a shrewd look as she racked a round into her pistol.

"So, you're pretty much just winging it," she said as we got to the door. I shrugged and nodded. "I can't tell you how confident that makes me feel," she said. I stepped through the open doors and turned to my left. Three aisles of mostly empty shelves occupied the floor. The end of the first row was clear, so I sidestepped and shined the tac light down the next row. Something shuffled across the floor, and I sidestepped again. The tac light shone on a pair of wide eyes that glowed in the narrow cone of its beam. I barely had time to register its

49

shriveled lips peeling back from its teeth before I pulled the trigger. Even with the suppressor on, the shot was loud in the confined space and I could feel the overpressure against my body. Behind me, Amy's pistol boomed twice.

"I got 'em," she called out.

"Mine's down, too," I said. "Let's see if there are any maps and get the hell out of here." The store had been stripped bare of pretty much everything except the rechargeable phone cards and ugliest of the cheap decorative crap. However, the rack with the maps on the counter was still full. Even the Slurp-it machine was gone. The tobacco section had been stripped bare, leaving only the bright ads for the various brands in place, and the liquor cabinet had been left just as empty. Amy grabbed a Nebraska state map on our way out the door. In the parking lot, the coast looked pretty clear, but I wasn't betting on that staying true for too long. I trotted to the road and saw a handful of zombies shuffling our way from either direction. From the headcount, I figured they weren't anything we couldn't handle, but the gunfire would probably draw more.

Across the road, I saw a blue sign that I'd missed as we'd pulled in.

State of Nebraska
Dept of Roads
Maintenance Yard

The gate was open, and a couple of Z's were shuffling around inside. But what had caught my eye was the gas tank and pump that was set inside. The pump was probably so much spare parts now, but if there was gas in the big tank, I could top off the truck's tank and fill the five gallon can the rest of the way without having to shoot a ton of zombies in the process.

"Get in!" I called out to Amy as I headed for the truck. Seconds later, I was closing the gate behind us, and Amy was out of the truck with her Ruger laid across the hood. The little rifle popped twice, and the two Zs dropped.

"Keep an eye on the road," I said as I went to the back of the truck and pulled out the hand siphon. The cap came off the top of the tank with a little elbow grease, and I ran the end of the long hose into the tank. The shorter hose went into the truck's tank, and I started pumping the piston handle. It was rated for about eight ounces per pump, so it took a few minutes to fill the tank all the way, and a few more to get the jerry can topped off. Once I was finished, I threw the siphon into the back of the truck bed, and set the fuel can back in with a lot more care, then I pulled the truck up until its nose was only inches from the gate.

"I've got this," Amy said as I went to get out. With a heave, she pulled on the gate as hard as she could. It slid open part way, and she pulled again. The second pull got the edge clear of the passenger side of the truck, and she ran for the door as the infected shuffled toward her.

"So," I said as she pulled the door shut. "Where to now?" She glared at me as I pulled out of the maintenance yard and turned back south.

"Give me a minute," she said.

"Well, shopping post apocalypse is a pain in the ass," I said as I drove past the shopping center. Infected were milling around in the parking lot, and they started shuffling our way as we passed.

"So is driving," she said. "We need to be about a mile north of here." I turned right at the first intersection I could find, and ended up headed down a concrete road that ran by a trailer park. The south side of the road was open fields, and the north side gave way to what had once been well manicured lawns. Two weeks without maintenance had taken a little of the cultivated edge from them, and the occasional bloodstain or lump of bloody goo on the road robbed it of its rural charm. After half a mile, things went from rural to rustic, spoiled by the occasional blank eyed face staring at us from a window. Graveled alleys that ran behind houses gave way to simple ruts in the grass. Then we came to a sign that said "Pavement Ends."

"Keep going," Amy said as we neared the straight line of pavement. "You're looking for 638 Avenue." I grunted an affirmative, hoping that the street sign was still there. Luck was with us, and I found myself turning north a mile later. I marveled at how clear the demarcation was between "town" and "country." Like the southern side of Auburn, the western edge was an all or nothing thing. One side, houses and streets, on the other, open countryside. Like Missouri, Nebraska was pretty in the fall, though October was feeling more like November just then. Then the town part fell away and we were traveling down what looked like any country road miles away from a town.

Pavement started again with no sign to warn us, and I pulled to a stop at an intersection with a broader road. Off to our right was an upholstery shop, and a cemetery loomed across the larger road to the left.

"This is it," Amy said, pointing to a green street sign across the way. "This is 136. Turn left." I pulled onto the highway, and wished for a radio station. At this point, even talk radio would have been a welcome distraction. Rural Nebraska was awful scenic, but after a certain point, the only thing that set it apart from Kansas was a slight roll to the landscape.

Two hours and a lot of turns later, we found a convoy of Army trucks and Humvees just north of a little town called Clay Center. They were pulled over on the south side of the road, and we could see bodies littering the parking lot of the big, tan building beside them. Worse still, there were dozens of infected walking around in the parking lot, along the road, and a few were wandering in the field on the north side of the road. The weapons on the convoy's vehicles were all pointed toward the building, and the tan walls were pockmarked with bullet holes. Only one of the vehicles showed serious damage. The lead Humvee was blackened and the roof and doors were gone. I could see them laying several yards away on either side of it.

"So, we just run on through, right?" Amy asked.

"No," I said. "We need to get into those trucks and see if they have a working radio, or find out where they're from. I figure this was a supply convoy that got overrun. Let's see what kind of supplies they were carrying. Who knows, maybe they have crates of M4s and ammo."

"And maybe we're risking our asses for three truckloads of tongue depressors and rectal thermometers," she said. "But, now I have to know. Damn it, Dave. So, what's Plan A?" I looked at the horde for a couple of minutes as I thought about it. Porsche and I had drawn off a horde of ghouls back in Springfield just by showing up and getting their attention. Once you had the attention of the infected, you had it until something else came along. Dumb as rocks, but persistent. The problem was that at the time, we hadn't planned on going back to Kickapoo High School, so we hadn't worried about drawing off all of the infected, and we weren't sure of the results. But, Captain Adams had checked my story out with the folks that were holed up there, so I figured it had to have been at least partially successful. Most of the infected there had been ghouls, though. I wondered how it would work with a mixed group.

"Plan A, they're all zombies, we show up, honk and get them to follow us for about half an hour, then come back a lot faster and check out the convoy. It worked in Springfield."

"And Plan B?"

"Plan B, some are zombies and some are ghouls, and we just do it twice, in different directions." I put the truck in gear and drove toward the church. The infected started to notice us when we got about a hundred yards away from the intersection, and I realized the flaw in my planning. I had planned on being able to make it to the cross road and turning north. As the zombies left the trucks, I realized they were a lot closer to it than we were.

"Dave, they're looking at us," Amy said with a note of concern in her voice. "They're in the intersection…did you happen to have a Plan C, or are we already making shit up as we go?"

"Yeah, we're playing speedchess," I said as I turned the wheel and sent the truck off the right side of the road. One thing I had to give Nebraska, they didn't seem to be big on fences in a lot of places. We made it through the shallow drainage ditch and into the field without getting stuck, then we were bouncing across the field, hoping the tires didn't get bogged down in the soft dirt. I pulled behind a house near the north bound road and turned to take the other drainage ditch at an angle. Once we hit pavement again, I let my hands relax on the wheel a little and turned to look back south. Infected came at us with glacier like speed. I looked over at Amy and shook my head.

"This…may take a while," I told her. I waited until they got within a few yards and gently pulled forward, making them follow us.

"This was a lot more exciting the last time you did it, wasn't it?" she asked a few minutes later.

"A little, yeah," I said. "There was a school full of kids involved, so there was a little more urgency to it, too."

"Which school?" she asked.

"Kickapoo," I said.

"I wonder if any of my friends are still alive," she said.

"Actually," I said after I goosed the gas to get a few more yards on the shambling horde, "I'm pretty sure they are. Aside from certain high value targets like yours truly, most of the military's efforts seemed to be centered on getting kids out of schools. And Glendale wasn't near a hospital."

"You know, after the stuff we found in that hospital in KC, I've got to wonder why they picked schools," Amy said. "I mean, people call kids the future of America and all that crap but it's not like a bunch of high school kids know how to save the world."

"That's pretty self-aware for a fifteen year old," I said. Amy shook her head and gestured for me to go.

"Dave, until we crashed in Kansas City, I didn't know how much I didn't know. I learned more stuff hanging out with you, Hernandez and Kaplan for one week than I did in a month at school. And that's after you taught me all the stuff you did when I got to stay with Mom. There's no way a bunch of kids in high school know squat about saving the world or fighting zombies or shit like that."

"Okay, I'll give you that," I said as we coasted to a stop. "But kids can learn."

"Yeah, that's what's got me worried," she said. "What the hell are they teaching them?"

"I don't know," I said. It had been in the back of my mind, but nothing more than a passing thought since I'd left Springfield. I'd had other things on my mind. Even now, it was mostly an abstract, since I didn't know much more than I did when shit hit the fan. "Sometimes, we just have to hold on to the question until the answer presents itself." I could tell by the look she gave me that she wasn't any happier with that than I was, but it was all I had.

Forty five minutes later, we were a good long way from the convoy. I sped up and took the first right turn I could, then two more. That brought us to the road we'd originally been on, and we approached the now mostly abandoned convoy. A couple of still-upright zombies were still wandering around, and half a dozen crawlers were inching our way. I drove over one as we approached, then went past the convoy so that the truck's rear was pointed at it. From behind, I could see that the rearmost truck was filled with rolls of concertina wire.

"So, are we shooting them from here?" Amy asked me.

"No, swords only. I don't want to advertise that we're here to everyone in ten miles." I pulled the Deuce from the back of the cab, and Amy grabbed her curved blade from its spot behind her seat. "Get the ones on their feet first, then we'll take care of the crawlers. The first one I came up on was blackened from the shoulders up, and his face was melted. Eyes and ears were burned away, leaving it with no way to find anything. It went down with a crunch as the Deuce cut into the side of its skull. I turned in time to see Amy pulling her blade out from under the second walker's chin. The crawlers were easier to take care of, mostly a matter of getting close enough to get a shot in from the neck up.

"Dave," Amy called out as I hit the last of the crawlers. She was standing over one of the crawlers, but she'd transferred her sword to her left hand and she'd drawn her pistol. I followed the direction she was pointing it, and found myself looking toward the back of one of the covered trucks. Dead infected were scattered around the rear of the truck. I switched hands with the Deuce and drew my Colt from the holster under my right arm. I gestured at her with my head, and she scurried over to take cover beside the nearest truck. I came up beside her and watched the back of the truck for a moment. The tarp moved slightly, and I saw the glint of light on metal.

"We might have a survivor," I said as I racked a round into the chamber.

"Not likely," Amy scoffed. "It's been two weeks. There's no way someone could survive that long in the back of a truck."

"Then cover me and hope I'm right," I said as I stepped out from beside the truck. I kept the Deuce down to my side, and the Colt pointed down but visible. "Hello in the truck. We aren't looking to hurt you or take your stuff," I raised my voice.

"Stop right there," a woman said from inside the truck. The barrel of a rifle slid out from the split in the middle of the back tarp. "Tell the girl to step out from behind the truck." I shook my head.

"Not gonna do that," I told her. "She's my kid. I'm not going to put her in your sights. I'm just trying to get to a radio. Could I use one of yours?"

"Batteries are dead," she said.

"Well, my truck's battery is working just fine. I could try to give you a jump in exchange for using one of your radios."

"Nope," she said.

"Then I just have one question. Where was this convoy from?"

"Hastings," the woman said. "We're from Hastings."

"Okay," I said. "Thanks. Look, we're heading that way. You're welcome to come with us. We'll wait for a couple of minutes." I took a couple of steps back and then to the side before I turned around and holstered my pistol.

"We're just leaving?" Amy asked when I walked past her.

"In a few minutes," I said as I went back to the truck. "We have at least part of what we need." I stopped long enough to cut a swatch of cloth from one of the crawlers and wipe the blade of the Deuce down before I put it back in the Kydex sheath.

"Wait!" we heard from behind us. We turned to see a woman in BDU pants and a green t-shirt stumbling toward us with her rifle slung. Her skin was pale, even more so against her dark hair. It made her eyes, almost as dark as her hair, stand out. "Please, wait." I put a hand out to Amy, a caution against drawing her pistol again.

"You're really going to Hastings?" the woman asked when she caught up to us. I nodded. "Then I'll go with you."

"Invitation's still open. I'm Dave, this is Amy," I told her. Up close, I could see the white lines of salt rings on her t-shirt.

"PFC Allie McKay," the woman said. "First Squadron, 134th Cav, Troop A."

"Is there anything you need to grab from the truck?" I asked her.

"Come take a look," she said. We followed, and she pulled the rear cover aside to reveal stacks of cardboard boxes labeled

"Humanitarian Daily Ration" and cases of bottled water. The wind shifted and I caught a whiff of excrement. On the south side of the road, I could see its source. To McKay's credit, she had managed to get her waste a pretty good distance from the truck. She'd used the empty ration bags to keep things contained and as close to sanitary as possible but two weeks in the same little space made for a lot of smell. More than one of the bags had come open as well. She climbed into the back of the truck, and I pulled myself up behind her.

Inside, I could see where she had cleared a place for herself in the middle of the truck's cargo. A collapsible bucket stood in the corner of the space, and a makeshift pallet made from stacked cardboard boxes was laid out along one side. Her BDU blouse was folded neatly atop one of the boxes, and she had set her helmet on top of it. Two empty magazines were stacked beside it, along with a spoon, towelettes in packets, a stack of napkins and a handful of other condiments from an accessory pack. Several foil pouches of crackers and spreads were laid out next to that. I'd only been outside the wire a few times while I was in Iraq, but I recognized the soldiers' habit of always keeping some food stashed away. In the Air Force, I was always sure of when and where my next meal was going to be, but in the Army, that wasn't always the case. Besides that, most soldiers burned a lot more calories than the average airman did.

"Welcome to my Fortress of Solitude," McKay said as she picked up the helmet and pulled her blouse out from under it. "Sorry it's such a mess, but it's the maid's day off. But hey, help yourself to anything from the kitchen. I've got plenty."

"Grabbing a couple of these boxes wouldn't be a bad idea. But do you mind if I take a look at your radios?"

"We only had one," she said as she stuffed the crackers and spreads into her cargo pockets. "And it's not even good for spare parts now."

"Was it in the lead vehicle?" I asked. She nodded and tucked the spoon into her breast pocket before she grabbed the two empty magazines.

"One of the guys got bit and started to turn, then the next thing we knew, a grenade went off inside it."

"I guess there are worse ways to go," I said as we each grabbed a case of water.

"Yeah, but they also had all the ammo. You wouldn't happen to have any five-five-six on you, would you? I'm fresh out."

"Actually, I do. Let's grab a few mags before we head out so we have something to put it in." Ten minutes later, we had ten extra magazines, and two cases each of the HDRs and bottled water loaded into the back of my truck. McKay climbed into the rear of the cab and stretched her legs out as she started to load the spare magazines.

"So, what happened back there?" I asked as we pushed on.

"We got orders to set up a road block north of Clay Center, and an aid station for refugees at the church," she answered after a few moments of thought. "We pulled up and saw all the people in the lot, so the LT gets out to go talk to them. I guess he figured they were waiting for us or something. And then, they all just run at him. And he just freezes up...just stands there. We don't want to rock and roll with him downrange, but Sergeant Crow, he tells us to shoot. So we did. Brought a lot of them down, too. But this one group, they get to the LT, and down he goes. Once that happens, we go full auto on 'em, mow 'em down like wheat, you know?" She stopped and took a shuddering breath before she continued. "But it's still not enough. They got to the Humvees first...that's about when the grenade went off. And then they got to the guys from the trucks. They just kept shooting at them...and after the first time, they got up...and then...they wouldn't fall down, no matter how many times we shot them. They just kept coming..." Her voice trailed off, and her gaze went to something distant, something only she could see.

"You have to shoot 'em in the head," Amy said softly. McKay's eyes focused on Amy, but I wasn't sure what she was actually seeing.

"Yeah, I figured that out," she said, her voice still distant. "I was in the back of the truck when they charged the LT. I just had my M4 with me. They didn't even issue us vests or packs. The other guys...they got out, and started shooting. Stan...he ran out, so he grabbed a shovel off the truck and started swinging. I should have got out. I should have been with them."

58

"You did the right thing," I said. "I don't know if you've looked around lately, but there aren't enough people with a pulse as it is. If getting corpse munched was the only way to save your buddies, sure, I can see that, but you're still human, and right now, that's like your primary MOS." She nodded and her expression changed.

"I'm sorry," she said with a soft smile. "I haven't talked to anyone for two weeks. So, do you know what's been going on anywhere else?" I let Amy take over the conversation from there, and focused on driving. Like most towns we'd seen, I figured there would be some attempt at containing the mass exodus with road blocks. So as soon as I found a set of railroad tracks that looked like they would lead into Hastings, I followed the gravel road the paralleled them for as far as I could go. Eventually, the road, named Technical Boulevard according to the lone green street sign I saw, veered away from the tracks. With no other option immediately open to me, I did the only thing I could do under the circumstances.

I went off road. To my surprise, the ride improved a little. We took the extremely scenic route for about a mile before the tracks veered north and I was forced to reconsider my brilliant plan. Before I got too deep in my own reasoning, I remembered that I had access to a better source for knowledge about the area.

"Allie, is there a set of tracks that goes through Hastings from east to west?" I asked as I coasted to a stop.

"Sure, but why not take the old right of way instead?" she asked as she pointed across the tracks. "It goes all the way into town, and it crosses behind all the places where we planned to put roadblocks." Where she pointed looked like a row of trees on the edge of a field, but when I pulled forward a few yards, it resolved into a tree lined path. I backed up and turned to bring the truck's nose perpendicular to the railroad tracks, then gently eased it across them, thankful for four wheel drive. The rear end scraped as we bounced over the second rail, and then we were rolling away from the tracks and toward the right of way. The ride was a little rougher, but it looked like a straight shot into Hastings.

When we finally ran out of open fields, we found ourselves emerging onto a street that ran by a park. Allie pointed across the road to where the right of way continued. It led us through the back side of the town's industrial district, past storage sheds and salvage lots, and all the way to another set of railroad tracks. I followed those west at Allie's direction, and turned back north on a street called Woodland. Stacks of PVC pipe in every size imaginable lined the roadway, then gave way to a storage business on one side and a line of repair shops on the other before it ended at a cross street.

"That's the armory," Allie said, pointing to a two story brick building with a chain link fence surrounding a lot on the side facing us and a white garage or storage building that butted up against the fence "It doesn't look like it's been-" she started to say, and then abruptly stopped as a man wearing black pants and a green flak jacket emerged from behind the storage building. Immediately, he brought an assault rifle up to his shoulder and opened fire. As soon as I saw the gun move, I pushed my foot down on the gas, and we burned rubber across the road and jumped the curb, then bounced over the concrete parking stops. Rambo ran out of rounds before we hit the curb, but he still managed to hit the truck a few times. We shot across the side lot, then across the road that ran in front of the armory before we hit grass again and found ourselves in a shaded park. More shots rang out behind us, but it seemed like most of them were killing any trees that dared to shelter us, though a couple of rounds hit the body of the truck with hollow sounding *thunks*. A beige building loomed up ahead, and I swerved to put it between us and the armory.

"I think someone took over the armory," McKay said.

"Yeah, I was getting that impression!" I yelled as I yanked the steering wheel to the right to miss a Humvee that was bearing down on our left side. The other vehicle hit its brakes as we swung through someone's yard and came back onto the street. I heard the chatter of a machine gun for about a second and saw chunks of asphalt fly in front of me and to my left. I swerved right and left to spoil their aim, but they didn't seem to be shooting at us.

"The gun jammed!" McKay said from behind me. In the rearview mirror, I could see her looking out the back window.

"Good," I said as I poured on the speed. More automatic fire came, and I reached out to push Amy down in the seat as I heard a few rounds hit the rear of the truck. Then the back end started vibrating and the Humvee gained ground as I lost speed. The sound of rubber slapping against asphalt and the truck frame beat an uneven rhythm as I tried to keep what little lead I had on our pursuers with a rear tire gone. Behind us, I could hear someone yelling triumphantly, and I promised myself I'd make them pay for that.

"We're going to have to ditch the truck," I said as the back end started slewing back and forth. "Once we stop, McKay, I need you and Amy to get to cover."

"Copy that," McKay said as she slid my M4 onto the seat beside me. "We'll cover you." She handed Amy the shotgun and chambered a round in her own rifle. Seconds later, the Humvee rammed us, and I almost lost control of the truck. As I tried to straighten the front end out, shots rang out behind us, and I heard rounds zip through the cab. Then a telephone pole filled the windshield and everything stopped except for me.

The next thing I knew, I was face first against something white, and I felt like I'd been kicked in the chest by a mule. I pushed back and found myself looking over a deflating airbag. Amy was shoving her way clear of hers, and McKay was slumped over the top of the seat with a red stain spreading across her back. I shoved McKay's rifle at her and groped for my own.

"Cover," I said through the cotton that seemed to be filling my mouth and head. "Get to cover." She grabbed the gun and opened the door of the truck as I fumbled for the latch to my door. Finally, I got it open and stumbled out. The ground swayed beneath me and I went down, the M4 clattering away from me as I caught myself.

"Man, look at this fucking loser," I heard someone say. The world moved around me as I tried to see who was talking, tried to find a target. "We seriously poned his ass."

"Watch this shit," another one said. Something hit me in the left side and knocked me rolling. I landed on my back and reached for the SOCOM. A chorus of expletives filled the air as I pulled the trigger. The gun bucked in my hand three times before I heard someone scream. Before I could pull the trigger a fourth time, one of them kicked my forearm, and the gun went flying. I reached for the Colt with my left hand, and a weight fell on my chest.

"Get his other fuckin' gun!" the first guy said as he grabbed my wrist. More of them fell on me, and one pulled the Colt from its holster. "Mother fucker ain't such hot shit now, is he?" Then his rifle butt hit me in the head, and things went black for a little bit. When I came to, my hands were behind my back, and one of my captors was squatting in front of me with the SOCOM in his hand.

"Aw, fuck, you shot one of the bitches," another guy whined.

"No big loss," the guy in front of me said. "There's another one around here somewhere. She couldn't have gone far. We'll put this fucker down and then we'll go get her."

"Asshole shot Craig. Put a fuckin' bullet in his skull." My head was clearing and I stayed quiet, trying to size the men around me up. The first thing that I realized was that "men" barely described them. Most of them looked young, either barely out of high school or in college. The one in front of me seemed to be the oldest, and I wouldn't have pegged him as older than twenty. Dark haired, pale and beady eyed, he struck me as the kind of kid who thought his video game exploits made him a bad ass.

"Yeah, shoot his ass, Damon," another guy said, This one was big, blonde and handsome, right up until I looked into his eyes. What I saw there was ugly. Beside him was a dark haired kid half his size. Where the blond guy was carrying an M4 and wearing a bandoleer of bullets across his chest, this guy had gone the edged weapon route, with a pair of knives on his hips, one strapped to his forearm and another sticking up from the top of a cowboy boot. He even carried a katana in his right hand. The only gun he deigned to carry was a big revolver on his right hip. Beside him was a kid in a dark colored hoodie with a green flak vest over it and an M4 slung across his back and another in his hands.

"Nah," Damon said. A slow smile crept across his face as he turned his head to look at the big guy. "I've got a better idea. Go get that bottle of bleach."

"What are you planning to do?" I asked as I ran the fingers of my right hand against my left wrist. "Get my whites sparkling clean?" My fingertips brushed steel, and I felt the dimple of the keyhole. If they had known the right way to cuff someone, they would have had my palms out and the keyhole up on both sides. I put my hand to the small of my back, but the revolver was gone. My hidden handcuff key, however, was still clipped to my belt loop.

"Not your whites," Damon said as another guy came trotting up with the Mossberg in one hand and a bottle of bleach in the other. "Fuckers like you need to die slow. So you're gonna drink some bleach."

"Yeah, drink the bleach!" the knife guy said.

"Go ahead, drink the bleach," the big guy chimed in with a big grin. The fifth guy, a lanky kid with his head shaved and the beginnings of a patchy goatee starting to sprout from his face, handed Damon the bottle and chuckled.

"Boy, that's original," I said as I pushed the key into the hole and slowly turned it. "But it isn't a good idea." I could feel the tension pressing against the key. A fraction of an inch was all it would take to free my hand, but Damon was too far away. I needed him closer.

"Maybe not for you," he laughed as he unscrewed the cap. "But for us, it's gonna be a fucking blast."

"No, it isn't," I said, willing him to come closer. "I know more uses for what's in that bottle than you do, and none of them are pleasant. So if I was you, I'd back up and get the hell out of here." That made them laugh, and Damon started to lean in toward me. I turned the key far enough to free my left wrist, and reached for him. His eyes went wide as I grabbed his flak vest and drove my forehead into his nose. As he stumbled back, I grabbed for the SOCOM and put him in front of me, right in his team's line of fire. The pistol slid free of his grip as I heard a loud gunshot. When I pushed Damon away from me, I saw two things I didn't expect. One, the lanky kid with the bad goat and my shotgun was falling backward with a hole in his chest, and two, the other three guys were scrambling for the Humvee. Damon scrambled away from me and ran for the driver's door of the Humvee. Bullets starred the Humvee's windshield and sparked off the hood as the crack of another gun peppered the air. Another shot rang out, and half of the big guy's head went away as he tried to open the passenger side door. His buddy in the hoodie grabbed his rifle and jumped in just as more shots slammed into the door. They backed away for a few yards, then did a sloppy turn and tore off down a side street. I looked over my shoulder to see who was shooting, because the gun I'd heard firing was no M4. An older black man in blue jeans and a denim jacket was walking toward me with a bolt action rifle raised to his shoulder. Behind him were two other men, one with a semiauto rifle and the other carrying a bolt action hunting rifle with a scope. A second later, the first man lowered his gun, then dropped his gaze to me.

"You all right, son?" he asked.

"I should be. Can't say the same about the lady in the truck, though," I said as I got to my feet and leaned into the cab. I was pretty sure I knew what I was going to find, but I put my fingers to McKay's neck anyway. To my surprise, I felt a weak pulse.

"Sorry about your girlfriend, son," he said.

"Don't be," I said as I grabbed my D.A.R.K. trauma kit from my belt. "She's still alive!"

Chapter 4
Cold Comfort
~ On wrongs swift vengeance waits. ~ Alexander Pope

"She's not my girlfriend," I said for what felt like the hundredth time.

"That's what your daughter said," George told me with a grin. "And I know, she ain't really your daughter." The man who'd led our rescue had some gray in his hair up close, and when he wasn't busy shooting people, he had an easy smile.

"He's adopted," Amy said. "But we think of him as family just the same." George's smile became a brief laugh.

"Well, Dr. Harper did the best he could, but she's still not doing too well," George said in his rich baritone.

"I'm a veterinarian," the round faced man beside him said. In his mid-thirties, Dr. Harper looked like he was borrowing a bigger man's clothes. His shirt seemed a size too big for him, and his pants were belted down two holes from the most worn notch. A pair of glasses was perched precariously in his thinning brown hair, and his eyes were almost hidden by a perpetual squint. "Though this isn't my first time dealing with gunshot wounds. But most of the time, I'm digging birdshot out of dogs. Still, the bullet lodged in her scapula. From what Coach Malcolm tells me, it must have been slowed down by going through the truck's frame, otherwise, it would have shattered her shoulder blade instead of just lodging in the bone. I'd need an X-Ray machine to tell how bad the bone is fractured, and I don't know what other damage might have been done. I'm…not sure I got all of the bullet out." I nodded silently and ran my hand through my hair. If McKay died, it would add another number to a count I *was* keeping track of. Unlike my zombie kill count, the number of people I'd either killed or hadn't saved was one I was keenly aware of. Not counting the crew of the chopper I'd managed to shoot down over Kansas City, my current estimate was fifteen people whose deaths were on my hands. It was a number I wasn't proud of, and I wasn't looking to add to it if I could avoid it.

Dr. Morris turned and headed back to the makeshift infirmary that had been set up in one of the Sunday School class rooms of the church we were in. Actually, calling it a church sold the place short. The place was a cathedral, though fortress would have been another good word for it. Outside, it was solid stone, and none of the windows was less than eight feet off the ground. The front doors were solid oak, and every side door that wasn't solid enough to stop a tank had been blocked off with pews, desks and tables. From where we sat in the cathedral itself, the place was huge. The pews had been turned into makeshift bunks, and I counted about twenty people up and moving around. From what I'd seen, there were another twenty or thirty more elsewhere in the building. As we talked, a man in a purple t-shirt and jeans walked over and sat down on the steps nearby. He wore his hair in tight dreadlocks under a bandana that kept them out of his face. He acknowledged us with a brief dip of his head, then seemed to turn his attention back to the rest of the cathedral.

"So, how did you guys keep this place from turning into a slaughter pit?" I asked George.

"We can thank Dean Stone for that, Lord rest her soul," George said somberly, his voice reflecting a little more of the Midwestern drawl that had only been on the edges of his words until now. "When people first started showing up, she set up an infirmary next door with the Baptist church. If anyone was sick or if they'd been bitten, she took them over there herself. Pastor Marks and her tended to 'em themselves. Healthy folks, they sent over here. All the way up to the end."

"Oh, I'm sorry," I said. George shook his head.

"Don't be, son. Her and Brother Sam died the way they lived, takin' care of their flock. The Lord'll look after 'em now. It's up to us to make sure they didn't do all that for nothin'."

"I take it you're not Episcopalian," Amy said. He shook his head and smiled.

"No, ma'am. I've been a Baptist since I was eight. But I'm not above taking refuge when refuge is offered, and take it from me, St. Mark's is about as safe a place as I've seen in Hastings. So, what are you gonna do now? Your truck's kinda busted up, though I think it could be fixed if you could get those back tires and rims replaced."

"Radiator's shot," I said. "Literally. There's no telling what other damage hitting that pole did to the engine. So, we have to get another vehicle, but we also need to get to one of the radios in the armory."

"That's not all that needs liberated from that place," the man who sat near us said. If George's voice was a pleasant baritone, this man's voice resonated in the shallow end of bass. He stood and walked over to us.

"Amen, brother," George said. "Damon and his crew took Dr. Crews prisoner a week and a half ago. If there's anyone who could take care of your friend, she's your woman. And she's not the only person they have. They're holding at least ten folks we know of, probably more."

"Who?" I asked.

"A few women, for obvious reasons, and some men for manual labor, we think. Who knows who all they have. Damon ain't all dumb. He knows his boys don't know what they need to stay alive for very long, but his answer is to force people to do what he wants."

"The boy is clever," the other man said. "At first, he used a CB to offer help to anyone who needed it. They'd capture anyone who showed up, take their stuff and kill anyone they didn't need. Then someone got wise to his wicked ways and started warning people about the armory. Now, he's setting himself up like a little feudal lord, offering protection, and the services of his captive doctor in exchange for tribute. His methods have earned him the loyalty of a few who think violence is strength."

"Who are you again?" I asked the new guy.

"Johnny Apocalypse," the dreadlocked man said with a smile. He put his hand out and we shook. "The voice of Radio Z."

"I heard your broadcasts when I was in Kansas City. I'm Dave." Amy introduced herself, and Johnny's gaze went back and forth between the two of us.

"Dave from Kansas City, and his daughter," Johnny said slowly. "Your last name wouldn't happen to be Stewart, would it?"

"My last name wouldn't happen to be anybody's business but my own," I said.

"Dave," Amy said. "Chill. It's not like he'd tell anyone."

"No, I understand," Johnny said as he raised his hands. "If he was the man I thought he was, it would make a target of anyone who knew him. And if he's the man I hope he is, I don't think he'd let that happen."

"Yep, you're Johnny Apocalypse all right," Amy said. "I thought you were just larger than life on the radio."

"No, little sister, I'm as large as life all the time," he replied. "Any more, there's no better way to be. But you, Dave, have the look of a man who's keen on doing something rash."

"Dangerous, maybe but not rash," I said after a moment's thought. "I always have a plan."

"At least one," Amy said. "You're about to go all rule twenty-three here, aren't you?"

"Can't say that it's entirely altruistic," I said. "We need to get to a radio. Otherwise, we're just wandering around out here without a plan and no one the wiser to where we are."

"So everyone wins," Johnny said with a sly grin.

"Pretty much. I'm going to need some things. First, I want to raid your janitor's closet. Is there a hardware store nearby?"

"Yeah, there's a Hammer'N Post just about three blocks south of here on West Second Street," George said. "We cleared it out a few days ago. I can send a team for whatever you need."

"You'll also need to hit a gardening store. I'll make you a list."

Four hours later, I was ready to start cooking. On the table in front of me were the bottle of bleach Damon had tried to make me drink, a five gallon water bottle, a bottle of Werx drain cleaner and a few other household items. The cathedral's modest kitchen had provided me most of the chemicals I needed, and on the table behind me was a respirator mask and a pair of swimming goggles. A camp stove and a pan were my first stops, though.

"So, what's this?" Amy asked as I stirred my concoction.

"Potassium nitrate and sugar. Two prime ingredients in a smoke bomb."

"Where did you learn how to make that?"

"High school chemistry class. Do me a favor and pull off some foil for me." She handed me a sheet of aluminum foil, and I started to fold it into a container.

"What's all the other stuff for?" she asked. "I mean, sulfur? Charcoal? Blanks for a nail gun?"

"All parts of things that go boom. Basic gunpowder is amazingly simple to make, once you know the right ratios and the right materials. And where to get all of it. Dangerous as hell, but still pretty simple. I don't need much, just enough to make a couple of small bombs. The chemical stuff…well, that's part of an object lesson for Damon and his boys." I handed her a pair of work gloves and pointed to a bag of charcoal. "Do me a favor, and start crushing about a pound of that down to as fine a powder as you can."

"Black powder, eh?" George asked from the kitchen door. "You've got to teach some of us that recipe." I turned to look his way. Johnny stood beside him, looking at the array of stuff before him.

"And smoke bombs, and a toxic gas…not shit you want to mix lightly. Assuming I survive this little raid, I'll tell you what I know. But right now, tell me what you know about the armory."

For the next few hours, my blood pressure was probably high enough to qualify for serious medication as I ground the ingredients for primitive gunpowder and got the rest of my improvised arsenal ready. By the time I was done, I had half a dozen Molotov cocktails ready to go, a big pressure bomb, a trio of smoke bombs and a black powder charge in a coffee can and two gas charges that just needed to be mixed and tossed.

"Okay, what time is it?" I asked as I straightened from inserting the fuse into the black powder charge. George looked at his wristwatch.

"Almost two in the morning," he said.

"Good. We just need a couple more people, and we can get this party started," I said.

"How many people do you need?" Amy asked after George left to find a couple of volunteers.

"At least five. The armory has doors on all four sides. The Molotovs will take care of keeping the side and back doors out of action at first, then we'll have to rely on old fashioned

69

suppression fire. Amy, I want you on my six, covering the front door."

"You're not going in there without me," she said. She put her hands on her hips, a pose that she had clearly inherited genetically from her mother.

"Surviving this would be a cinch compared to facing your mother if she ever found out I *deliberately* took you into a firefight," I said.

"And you think you can stop me?" she asked.

"Short of tying you up…not really. Just bear with me." George came back in with three other men. One of the men was carrying what I recognized as an SKS assault rifle, and the other had a deer rifle. George's rifle turned out to be an old Mosin-Nagant. In addition to the men I'd seen with him earlier, Johnny had tagged along.

"You're going to need something a little bigger than a handgun for what we're doing tonight," I said, pointing to the pistol on his hip.

"I'm not much of a fighter," Johnny said. "I'm going to be your witness. Somebody's gotta tell your story."

"Johnny, we already talked about how dangerous that would be," I said. He shook his head and gave me a broad smile.

"I'm not gonna use your name, Dave. But I am going to tell the world what you did. People need hope, and something like this will give 'em that in spades."

"Assuming I survive," I said. "So, here's the plan." They listened as I laid everything out for them. It didn't take long. As plans went, it was pretty simple. Less than twenty minutes later, we were on our way. It took us almost an hour to cover the ten blocks to the armory. The moon was at the last quarter, providing just enough light to see by once we let our eyes get used to the light. The dead were out, and we had to bring down a handful of them at an intersection with our blades. George's men looked at Amy with a little more respect once they watched her put her blade through a zombie skull. Finally, we reached our destination. George stayed with us while the other two went to take up their positions.

"Remember," I said to George fifteen minutes later. "Light 'em up when the shooting starts."

"And come in when Amy blows the whistle. Got it."

"Yup," I said, then turned to Amy and put my radio's earpiece in. "Remember, shoot and move. We go on your first shot." She did the same, and headed into the park while I crept up to the edge of the house on the corner and waited.

It seemed like forever before I heard the first crack of her Ruger going off. Someone cursed, and George and I rushed forward. He took cover behind a tree and light the gasoline soaked rag on his first Molotov while I kept sprinting for the corner of the building. The back of the building lit up as the first Molotov went off, and George's arced through the air as I closed on my objective. The night lit up behind me as I made it to the wall and crouched looking away.

"What the fuck was that?" someone called out.

"Get the night vision goggles!"

"Open fire! Shoot 'em!" Muzzle flash and the sound of gunfire erupted around the corner from me as Damon's crew poured lead into the darkness. I opened the top of the water container and up-ended the bottle of Werx into it. The six reactants inside rattled as I screwed the cap back on and shook it. Another crack came from the park, and someone cried out in pain. Another crack, and I heard the whine of a ricochet while I dumped the ammonia in with the bleach and hastily recapped the bottle. The sound of the two liquids sloshing was covered by more gunfire. Seconds later, I heard the call of "Reloading!" In the fitful light from the Molotov, I looked at the two bottles. The pressure bomb was starting to swell, but the gas mixture hadn't caused a very noticeable change in the bottle's shape. So far, so good. Neither was in danger of blowing up on me. I took the smoke bomb and my lighter out, then lit the fuse. More shots came from the park, now more quickly. Again, the boys behind the sandbagged entrance emptied their magazines at nothing, and I tossed the smoke bomb.

It went off a second before they ran their mags dry, and by the time the first one of them called out that they were reloading, there was a plume of thick gray smoke billowing up.

"What the fuck is this shit?" one yelled. Light flared behind me as George's second and last Molotov went off. With the renewed light, I could see a white vapor starting to form at the top of the water bottle. It was time to throw the pressure bomb. Under the cover of the smoke, I went around the corner and tossed the bottle over the top of the sandbags, then dropped flat. Gunfire erupted over my head, then cries of alarm.

"What was that?"

"Throw it back!"

"I got it!" Half a second later, the pressure in the bottle exceeded its strength, and it blew apart, sending boiling, corrosive liquid flying. I lit the fuse on the powder charge as the first screams tore through the night, then chucked it over the sandbags and scurried back to the corner. No one seemed to notice it amid the chemical burns, and it went off like a charm. I pulled the respirator up over my face and pulled the goggles into place.

When I came back around the corner, the smoke was clearing. Sandbags were tumbled onto the ground, and only moans reached my ears. The glass door had been blown off its hinges, and almost nothing but broken glass and wisps of acrid smoke stood between me and the interior of the armory. I tossed the deforming chlorine bottle into the hallway then stood to the side and unslung the Mossberg. I heard it bounce once, then the deep *boom* of it rupturing came from inside. After a few seconds, I came around the corner and found myself in a reception area that opened onto a hallway. A tumbled lantern lit the room. Movement came from my right, and I turned the shotgun toward it. It bucked in my hands as I found a target, and the guy went down. I heard footsteps coming my way, then coughing and cursing. I pointed the Mossberg down the hallway, pumped a fresh round into the chamber and sent three more blasts down the hallway. My effort was rewarded with a scream, and I put my back to the wall and loaded four more rounds into the tube.

Muzzle flash lit the hallway and plaster flew as someone opened fire from down the hallway.

"Got your six," I heard in my earpiece, then a fresh scream joined the chorus.

"They've got the doors covered!" someone called out from deeper inside.

"We got night vision!" I heard Damon yell. "We fucking own the night!"

"Damon, someone's inside, man!" I heard from nearby. "They shot me!"

"We got fucking body armor!" Damon yelled back. I peeked around the corner and didn't see anyone.

"I'm bleeding man!" the guy close to me screamed. Then he coughed, and staggered into view, and I aimed for his hips. He flopped and writhed as he let out a high pitched squeal.

"They're using some kind of nerve gas!" one yelled as I scrambled down the short hallway. Ahead of me I could see a dim light in an open area. The guy I'd shot was just outside the hallway.

"Turn out the lights!" Damon yelled. As darkness descended, I reached out and grabbed the wounded man and dragged him into the hallway with me.

"He's got me!" the wounded man screamed. "Help!" I pulled his NVGs off and slipped them down over my face.

"Shut the fuck up," I said and hit him in the jaw with the butt of the shotgun. More coughing started to come from deeper inside the building.

"Hey, Damon," I called out. The respirator robbed me of a lot of volume, but I was sure Damon and his crew were listening real close now. "Remember me? I'm the guy who broke your nose earlier."

"I'm gonna kill you, motherfucker!" he yelled back. I risked a look into the open area and saw four Humvees. Damon and his crew were spread out, hiding behind the Humvees and crouched in doorways. Only a few of them had NVGs or flak jackets on. Most of them were only carrying sidearms and stumbling around like they'd just woken up.

"Yeah, good luck with that. Do you smell that? That's one of the things you can do with bleach if you know what you're doing. You feel that burning sensation in your nose and throat? That's what it feels like when the mucus membrane first starts to break down. Your eyes will go next."

"Bullshit!" Damon called back. "Open the garage door." I heard the creak of the door lifting, and a fresh breeze filled the room. With the air starting to clear, I pulled the respirator and goggles off and readjusted the NVGs. It was time to turn their strength against them. I reached into my vest and pulled out a road flare. It glowed red when I activated it, and I heard several surprised cries as NVG screens flared. When I threw it, I could see several heads turning. I pointed the shotgun toward a doorway where one of the gawkers was and pulled the trigger as I rushed forward. Gunfire erupted on the hallway, but by then it was several feet behind me. Now I was into the room, and out of the choke point.

As the first salvo stopped, I hit the ground and slid a couple of feet. From my vantage point, I could see a pair of feet on the far side of a Humvee, so I brought the shotgun up and sent nine double ought buckshot pellets at them. The guy hit the floor howling, so I pumped another round into the chamber and pulled the trigger again, then rolled to an office door and pulled three shells from my vest.

"Where the fuck is he?" someone asked. As if in answer, a rifle boomed, and more cries erupted.

"He's behind us!" someone yelled.

"Shut up," Damon yelled as another shot rang out. "That came from outside. Close the garage door!"

"I'm in," I whispered into the mic.

"Right behind you," I heard Amy say. I grabbed an office chair and pulled it toward me, then leaned out and shoved it toward the next door. I had barely pulled back behind cover before two guys opened fire on it. They ran dry at almost the same time, so I stepped out and shot the one who was standing in the door of the next office down, then shot at the one behind the next Humvee. I heard the second guy curse as I kept moving, hoping against logic that this crew wasn't as good in a real firefight as they might have been at the virtual kind. Another shot boomed from outside, and I heard a body drop.

"Get that fucking door closed!" Damon yelled. I came up on another guy taking cover in an office, and barely managed to get the first shot off. He squeezed the trigger on his M16 and sent a three round burst zipping past me before he stopped twitching. Then I was past the second Humvee and had a clear shot on the guy who had just made it to the door. I shot him in the ass. Then I heard the first shot from the hallway.

"Who the fuck was that?" someone cried out.

"That would be the rest of my team," I lied. "You're running out of people, Damon. How many more are you going to let die before you give up?"

"Fuck you!" Damon yelled back.

"I already took your one advantage from you," I said as I tossed another flare into the room. "You've got what, five or six guys left?" A shot rang out from the other side of the room and someone else started screaming. "Sorry, four or five guys left?" I pulled a shell from my vest and went to load it. As I was about to slide it into the loading port, something knocked the Mossberg out of my hand. I jumped back as a sword blade sliced through the air where I had just been.

"Don't shoot him!" the sword wielding badass yelled as I backed away from him. "He's mine!" He thrust the tip toward me and gestured toward the middle of the open area opposite the Humvees.

"Seriously. Have you *ever* read the Evil Overlord's list?" I asked as I backed into the open.

"Draw your blade!" he said.

"Guess not," I said as I drew the Deuce. As close as he was, I probably couldn't get the SOCOM out before he skewered me. For the moment, I had to play along. He smiled as the blade cleared the sheath, and I knew he'd never fought against anyone with any serious training. Whenever I faced new opponents in the SCA, none of them were happy when they saw that they were fighting a lefty. Sir Ginsu of Cuisinart, on the other hand, didn't look upset or even mildly irritated at my unholy southpaw ways. He dipped his blade to me and stepped back, then dropped the point to the concrete and dragged it in a semicircle in front of him. I couldn't help myself. I hung my head and shook it.

"Kid, you're not Blade. Hell, you're not even Wesley Snipes."

"My name is Razor," he said as he spun his blade in a broad arc. That part he seemed to know how to do. "It's the last name you'll ever hear."

"Razor," I said, suppressing a laugh. "My name is Dave Stewart. You killed my truck. Prepare to die." I settled into a ready stance and waited for him, my eyes on the middle of his chest.

"You're quoting The Princess Bride?" he asked as he started to circle to my left.

"I thought it fitting, considering the comedic terrain," I said as I stepped to my left, inside his circle. The move caught him off guard and he stepped back, crossing his feet as he did. He tried circling the other way, and I side stepped into his movement again. He feinted at me, but his center of gravity never changed, so I stayed still. He tried it again, but never committed to a full thrust, so I didn't move. Finally he made a serious thrust, and I moved my blade to the left a few inches, keeping the point in place on my center line. The move knocked his attack away from my body, and he withdrew. A split second later, he came at me again with a bevy of rapid fire blows.

One of the things Willie had been teaching me while we had been in KC was a defensive technique called the cone of power. The sword itself barely moved, the point staying nailed in place along the centerline of the body. By moving the lower part of the sword like a pendulum, all it took was a few inches of movement to cover one side of the body from head to hips. Razor's katana bounced off the Deuce with a series of discordant clangs, none of his strikes coming close to me.

"What are you waiting for?" he yelled after he broke off the attack. "Fight damn it!"

"I just want you to feel you're doing well," I quoted. "I hate for people to die embarrassed." He brought his blade up over his head and dropped into a sloppy fighting stance. It was a mediocre imitation of a kendo stance, and I'd been on his side of it before. In my case, I'd been facing an SCA knight using a rattan sword. All I'd been betting on it was my pride.

"I'm going to take your sword after I kill you and cut your head off with it," he snarled. "There is no defense against this stance."

"Unless your opponent has studied his Agrippa," I said as I came forward. "Which I have." As I finished the line, I lunged forward and snapped my blade at him, aiming for his right wrist. He had three options. He could defend and survive, he could attack and die, or he could flinch. Although attacking would end up killing him, though there was an outside chance he could take me down with him. Defending would save both his life and some of his pride.

He flinched. It saved his life, but it probably killed his standing with his few surviving friends. Whether it was pride or some remaining belief that speed and flash were a good substitute for skill that drove him, I couldn't be sure. He slashed at me a couple of times, then wove his sword in front of him in glittering figure eight, the red light of the flare glinting off his blade as he spun it around and came at me with a yell on his lips. I'd played his game long enough; I was done with this fight.

"Enough!" I bellowed as I swung the Deuce straight down. It caught his cheap katana on the upswing and sheared through the blade near the suba. The blade spun though the air and embedded itself in a door. "Yield," I said to Razor as I put the point of my sword a few inches from his throat. "Don't make me kill you." His face twisted into a snarl, but he tossed the broken sword away. I came up out of my stance and inclined my head to him, then brought the Deuce up in a salute. He looked like he'd swallowed a lemon whole, but he nodded. Without taking my eyes off of him, I reached up and slid the sword back into its sheath, then turned halfway away from him and released the strap on the SOCOM.

"And don't think about trying to stab him in the back," Amy said as she stepped into view from behind a Humvee with her gun trained on Razor. "That shit never works." To my left I could see Damon and the kid in the hoodie standing by an office door. Two more of his crew were crouched over the prone form of a third, their expressions grim. Johnny came out behind Amy, his pistol out but pointed down.

"Is this your fuckin' team?" Damon said as he looked us over.

"Nope, there's more," I said.

"Bullshit," he said and drew his pistol. Mine came up at the same time and we stared at each other over the barrels. "Put the gun down bitch, or I shoot his ass," he said as he turned his head toward Amy without taking his eyes off of me.

"Dave?" she asked.

"Rule fourteen," I reminded her.

"Gotcha," she said, and I could hear the feral grin reflected in her voice.

"I said put it down bitch!" Damon said again, his voice louder. "Don't fuckin' push me, or I swear I'll blow his-"The rest of his final words were drowned out in the report of the SOCOM. When my barrel came back down, Damon was sprawled on the floor, and the wall behind him was black with blood splatter. Slowly, I turned the gun on the hoodie kid. His eyes were wide and he was shaking hard enough that I could even see it in the fading red light.

"Drop your gun, kid," I said. His M4 clattered to the floor. The other two set their weapons down as well.

"Is that everyone?" Amy asked.

"I think so," Razor said. "I think you killed everyone else." With Razor's assessment, I pulled out the whistle George had given me and blew the all clear code we'd agreed on, three short and one long tweet. While we waited for George and the other two men, I ordered Razor to take off all the cutlery and we secured the rest of the survivors.

"What's rule fourteen?" Razor asked as I pulled the zip strips closed around his wrists.

"Basically, don't point a gun at someone unless you're ready to pull the trigger." His Adam's apple bobbed as he swallowed, then he looked dead ahead and went very still. I could hear George and the others come in the front door. Johnny went to meet them. Now that I had a second to look around I could see that the outside edge of the drill floor was actually pretty crowded. Cardboard cases of MREs and HDRs were stacked near the garage door, with tables and piles of gear set up along the far wall.

"Dave," I heard George call out as he and Johnny headed my way. "We've got incoming."

"Dead or alive?" I asked.

"The dead kind. Probably heard the commotion and decided to come check it out."

"Are the other doors still pretty solid?" I asked.

"Hell yeah," he said. "We just scorched the paint is all. The only one that's damaged is the front door."

"You think we've got enough time to get a good barricade up?"

He shook his head. "Not enough people, not enough material and nowhere near enough time. Hell, we'd probably make enough noise trying to reinforce the door that they'd zero right in on us. They might pass us right by."

"I can help," Razor said. I was going to have to ask him to tell me his real name before long.

"Nope, sorry. That whole 'trying to kill me' thing you did makes me not trust you a little," I said.

"They're drawn to noise," he said, pressing on. "But not just anything. It has to be sounds that remind them of people."

"He's got my attention," Johnny said.

"Music seems to work pretty good, but the best stuff is where there's people singing or talking. They really go agro on that. We used a CD player in a cage as a Z magnet when we wanted to raid a place. Just set it down, push play and watch 'em all come out. Used to make noobs do the dead run for their initiation." We all exchanged looks, and Amy shrugged.

"You still have the CD player?" she asked.

"In there," he said, nodding toward one of the offices.

"Why are you suddenly so helpful?" Johnny asked after she left.

"Because the Zs don't care who they munch on," he said. "They get through that door, I'm just as dead as you fuckers. At least this way, I have a chance." I looked at Johnny and George, and they both nodded, so I went to the back of one of the Humvees and grabbed a folding e-tool.

"What's your name?" I asked as I sorted through the pile of knives on the hood of the Humvee closest to him. "You're real name."

"Chris," he said. I picked out a full tang Bowie knife and a bayonet. The Army's M9 bayonet was a decent knife for both survival and combat, and the Bowie had the length and weight to handle a fight. But for zombie killing, my money was on the e-tool. He got to his feet once I cut the zip strips free, and dutifully followed me over to the tables. I grabbed several MREs and started cutting them open, dumping the contents onto the table and field stripping them. With the cardboard removed, the heating elements and some of the condiment packages tossed, I got nine MREs into five packages. I tossed those and a few water bottles into a rucksack.

"There's three days' worth of food in there," I said when I handed it to him. "If you're smart, you'll grab one of those shelter halves over there, too. Use the e-tool to smash heads. And next time you think about getting a sword, pick up a machete instead." Amy came up and set a wire mesh cage on the table with a CD player secured inside.

"I replaced the batteries," she said. "And I changed out the CD for a Nickelback album. That way you don't lose anything worth listening to." I held my tongue, not sure if liking some of their songs made me too uncool or not. He grabbed one of the shelter halves and tied it to the bottom of the ruck, then slid it onto his back and headed for the front.

"Okay, Chris," I said when we were just inside the door. "I figure this doesn't exactly even things up between us, but it's a good start. But if I ever see you again and you draw a weapon on me, I will kill you."

"What if I don't?" he asked.

"I guess that'll depend on what we're both doing," I said. He let one side of his mouth quirk up and nodded. "One last thing before you go. A sword is a weapon of honor. Think about that before you pick one up again." His lips tightened into a thin line, and he gave me a long look before he spoke.

"Okay," he said. Without another word, he took off across the street. A few moments later, I heard music start.

"Do you think he'll do it?" Johnny said from behind me as the music faded into the distance.

"You shouldn't walk up behind people like that," I said. "Do what? Think about the whole honor thing? I don't know. I hope so."

"Me, too," he said. We turned and headed back inside.

The people Damon's crew had taken captive were out when we made it back to the drill floor, and someone had shut the garage door. Another guy was face down on the floor, with one of George's men binding his hands behind his back none too gently.

"We found him hiding in with the hostages," George said as he came toward me with a woman beside him. Her short, dark hair didn't hide the bruises on her face, and her right eye was still puffy and swollen from a recent blow.

"Sneaky bastard. Strip him down to his underwear," I said loudly enough for everyone to hear. "Cut his shirt off if you need to."

"Hey, let us go and we'll help you out, too!" the hoodie kid said as we passed him.

"Screw that, your buddy volunteered first," George said. "You didn't speak up until you thought there was something in it for you. No deal, kid."

"We need to at least get a barricade in that hallway," I said. George nodded and the woman standing beside him stepped up.

"Coach Malcolm can take care of the barricade," she said, her brown eyes flicking back and forth as she looked me over. "You need to sit down and let me treat that wound before you pass out from blood loss."

"What wound?" I asked.

"That one," she said, pointing one slim finger at my stomach. I looked down to see a hole in my vest, with a red stain around it. Pain flared along my side when I took a breath, and I felt a sudden chill creep up the back of my neck.

"That's gonna leave a mark," I said. My hands shook as I started to remove the vest.

"Are you always a smartass?" she asked as she reached out to help.

"Only when shit gets bad," Amy said.

Journal of Maya Weiss

October 29

I met the people Dave sent from Kansas City a couple of days ago. They had to be the train Johnny Apocalypse heard the night before. Even though I knew they wouldn't be with them, I kept looking for them, hoping I'd see them. A few had spent time with them, especially Willie and the two Marines, Hernandez and Kaplan. Everyone seemed to know something about them, though. I'm going to have to talk to Dave about what he's turning my daughter into. These people keep track of zombie kill count like baseball fans keep track of batting averages and home runs, and while Dave's is pretty high, it's Amy's that worries me. Especially since Dave and she have the most "special" kills. It wouldn't be so bad if all of this was for some stupid video game, but this is real life and death.

Enough of that. We loaded our little convoy onto the train and went as far west as we could. The end of the line was a town called Veteran, Wyoming. The tracks actually kept going, but they looped back north and east after Veteran. We camped there and tried to plan our route. These are the days when I miss the map function on my phone. But, Nate already had a plan. The maps in the Land Masters had routes marked on them that would get us to his place. It took us most of the day, but tonight, we're camping about 25 miles from Nate's place. Hopefully, tomorrow will see us safe.

Radio Z is back on the air tonight. Johnny started off with Black Magic Woman, then played Halestorm's cover of Bad Romance and followed them with more of Dave and my favorite songs. After a few songs, he stopped and I could hear music playing in the background. "Hear that, America? That's the sound of courage and mercy. Last time, I told you I was going to go check out a town I'd heard about that had some troubles. Well, I found it. And I found heroes, too. They took care of their troubles, with the help of a wandering survivor. Make no mistake, some people died tonight; justice is harsh out here in the wasteland. But I also saw a man show mercy when he could have taken a life, and I got to see a man get the chance to turn his life around. I watched a man risk his life to save a stranger, and I watched a doctor who had just worked on one patient brave the streets in the dark to save another one who needed her. Yeah, I found a whole group of heroes. But I found one in particular. He says he's just another survivor, like anyone else. But I don't buy it. This dude fights the good fight. But you want to know the best part? This is gonna break your hearts, kids. After the dust settled, the good people here in Hastings asked our survivor to stay around. But our boy is dead set on makin' his way back to the woman he loves. Now ain't that sweet? So, for all you out there tonight listening in, this show is dedicated to the lady that he's trying to find. I hope she's safe. So, here's to heroes in love, boys and girls." He played Magic Man after that, and then, he went off the air.

He didn't use Dave's name; he didn't have to. The whole broadcast was like one long, musical love note just for us.

Chapter 5
Marching Orders
~ I see my path, but I don't know where it leads. Not knowing where I'm going is what inspires me to travel it. ~ Rosalia deCastro

"The psychosomatic shock was more dangerous to you than the gunshot wound," Dr. Crews said as she finished changing the bandage on the wound. "It just went through some adipose tissue and came out the other side. Nothing too serious, as far as gunshot wounds go."

"Doesn't feel that way," I said. "Feels like I got kicked in the gut by a mule." My abdomen hurt in front and in back, and Dr. Crews hadn't had much to work with in the way of anesthetic. I hadn't been the ideal, stoic patient, either.

"If you can complain, I think you'll make it. You're about as bad as my other patient," she said.

"So, McKay's going to be okay?" Amy asked. Her face brightened as she waited for the answer.

"She'll live, but I'm not sure how much use she's going to get back in her left arm. If I had access to a physical therapist for her, and all the facilities I needed, I'd say she'd get almost eighty percent. Now, though?" She paused and shook her head. "Now I can't even begin to guess."

"How long am I going to be laid up?" I asked as I pulled my new t-shirt down.

"Technically, you can get up now, but I wouldn't recommend it." She frowned at me as I tried to push myself up. With Amy's arm under my shoulder, I was able sit up. Getting my feet on the floor was a minor victory of its own, and walking to radio room felt like winning a marathon. The Spitfire radio terminal weighed less than twenty pounds but as I lugged my prize to the workbench in the room, I felt myself flagging. By the time I got it out, I had to have Amy carry it to the one of the three Humvees that they had been using to ferry people and equipment between the armory and St Mark's. The fourth one had taken the other two rounds that had been fired at me.

"So, we have our radio," Amy said as I followed behind her. "What now?"

"I need to find a satellite and get the antenna aligned. So I need a rooftop."

"You need to get to the roof?" George asked from the driver's seat.

"Beats setting it up in the parking lot," I said as I climbed into the passenger seat.

"I'll get you up there then," he said over the truck's rumble. Amy climbed in the back and pulled the door closed. He pulled out of the garage and gave the big diesel some gas as we pulled clear of the gate, taking the turn a little wide to make sure the trailer hitched to the back cleared the fence. Outside, the first hints of dawn were starting to creep into the sky ahead of us. Bodies littered the road, infected that fell victim to the front grill of the Humvees or their tires. As we drove along, I could see the not-so-dead ones shuffling around on side streets. We passed one that was facing east with its head tilted back. I watched it as we came up on it, and it turned away from the sunrise and began to wander toward one of the houses. Others seemed to be doing the same thing.

"Where are they going?" Amy asked, saying aloud what I had been wondering.

"Out of the sun," George said. "You don't see many out when the sun's up, not sure why. Some folks think it's because they're allergic to it or something. But they're not vampires. I've never seen one of 'em burst into flames in the sunlight. Near as I can figure, they just don't like it."

"Maybe it's something to do with the melatonin and serotonin thing Ruth was talking about," Amy offered. "I think melatonin's the one called the darkness hormone, something about too much light keeping people from getting enough of it."

"Blue light," George said with a short laugh. "My wife used to wear this pair of yellow glasses every night before bed. She said they were supposed to block blue light and help her sleep hormones." More and more infected were moving off the streets, and I wondered if the stage one ghouls were the same way. Moments later, we were pulling into the parking lot beside the church. I got out and walked the short distance between the Humvee and the gate into the walled courtyard beside the cathedral. George led us to the door into the kitchen and pushed me toward a chair at the table.

"I can walk," I said as he put his hands on my shoulders and gently pushed me into the seat.

"I know you can," he said, completely ignoring my protest otherwise. "But you lost a little blood, and Doc Crews said to get plenty of fluids and high protein foods into you. She gave me a list, and you're not moving from that spot until you eat."

"Spinach, beans, orange juice and meat," Amy said. "I really want to see him try to choke down a can or two of spinach."

"I can help with the food part," I said as I tried to get to my feet.

"You already went and got yourself shot," George said. "What makes you think you're safe in a kitchen full of knives and hot surfaces? Sit your ass right back down." I let myself sink back down into the chair and forced myself to sit still while they cooked. Somewhere along the way, my eyes closed and I dozed off, because the next thing I knew I was jerked awake as my right leg twitched. I let my head droop again, and before long I was greeted by the sound of a bowl being set on the table. True to the list she'd quoted, Amy and George had put together a full meal from a combination of MREs and canned goods. To my surprise, even the spinach tasted almost as good as chocolate and I was scraping the bottom of the plate too soon for my stomach's liking.

Once the food was gone, I slipped out of the kitchen and found the radio. Someone had unloaded it from the truck and left it near the front of the pews. Inside the box was what I needed almost as much as the radio itself: the instruction manual. I had used the Spitfire radio terminal before, but it had been a few years.

"Welcome to the exciting new world of military radio," I said under my breath as I moved to the nearest pew and sat down. "Your AN slash PSC5 Spitfire Radio Terminal and You will provide you with hours of entertaining reading as you learn about exciting topics like frequency presets, COMSEC key loading and other military abbreviations." Like most military manuals, this one was very dry. My head started bobbing before I'd gotten to the bottom of the first page.

The next time my eyes opened, I was looking up at the cathedral's ceiling. The light was streaming in from the stained glass windows in the front of the church, and somehow that was important. When I stretched, my belly reminded me that a bullet had just gone through it with a pretty sharp jolt of pain and my yawn turned into a sharp exhale of discomfort. Sitting up was an expedition to new kinds of suffering, so I turned on my side and pushed myself upright with my arm. Facing the east end of the church, I realized why the pretty colors at the front of the church were important. That meant the sun was on the west side of the building. Judging by the angle of the sunbeams, it was well past noon.

"You don't snore as loud as mom says you do," Amy said from behind me. Twisting too far in either direction didn't seem like a good idea, so I stood up and turned around. At least that seemed a little easier than it had been a few hours ago. Amy was stretched out on the pew behind me, with her pack and weapons stacked at her feet. She had one of the books we'd traded for open on her chest, one finger stuck between the pages to keep her place. My gear was stacked neatly on the pew in front of me, with the notable addition of an ammo box and a stack of magazines next to the M4.

"Maybe getting shot fixed that," I said. "Crap, I slept too long." I grabbed the manual from beside my pack and sat back down. The light lasted through the last page, but I didn't beat sunset by much. I unpacked the radio by lantern light, and by the time I got it ready to go, night had fallen. I followed George to a small circular stairwell hidden in the south wall, and we found ourselves climbing onto the tower roof, one of the highest points around. Finding a working satellite took me almost an hour, but the signal came in strong and clean, and I loaded in the COMSEC key.

"Jayhawk, this is Magic Man," I said into the mic. "Come in, Jayhawk." I waited, imagining a hundred terrible possibilities with every second that passed.

"Hoo-ah, Magic Man. This is Jayhawk, it's good to hear your voice. You just made me a million dollars." Nate Reid's voice was a little tinny over the radio, but it was still the enthusiastic rumble I remembered from hours of talks at his kitchen table.

"Never bet against me," I said with a smile. "Speaking of people you shouldn't bet against, did Maya make it there yet?" My heart started pounding in my chest as I waited for him to answer.

"She made it in this morning," Nate said. "And she brought about 300 house guests with her. Plus your cat." I laughed, so relieved that I wasn't sure how I kept from either deflating on the spot or exploding.

"Yeah, watch out for Leo…he'll tear you up something fierce," I said. "I guess you heard about me and Keyes."

"Yeah, Shaw's right hand. You don't do anything halfway, do you?" he asked.

"Well, if you're going to do something, do it well," I said. "So, right now, I'm pretty much radioactive. After this, I'm going to find a hole, pull it in after me and go dark for a couple of weeks. So, if Maya's around, Amy and I would like to talk to her."

"Roger that," Nate said. "I have someone on their way to get her. Since you're off the reservation, there's something we'd like you to do."

"Well, I'll have to check my busy social schedule," I said. "I have golf with the President, then the regatta at the yacht club after lunch. I'll see what I can do. But who's this we you're talking about?"

"Mr. Stewart," another voice came over the handset. "This is Colonel Shafer. Son, I already owe you more than one drink for helping us back in Springfield. Way I hear it, there's a few Marines and civilians who owe you and Maya their asses, too. But I'm afraid I'm going to have to add to the tab."

"What do you need, sir?" I asked, forcing a dozen questions to the back of my mind. "Bear in mind, I have a teenage girl with me, so firefights are right out. And dances. Especially dances." Amy slapped at my arm at that and I gave her what was supposed to be a stern look.

"No, I'm pretty sure no one is going to be shooting at you. We just need you to go retrieve some data about the Asura virus. Should be pretty much Marine proof. All you need to do is go in, grab anything pertaining to Project: Home Shield and get your ass back here."

"I can do that," I said. "Where am I going?"

"It's an old COG installation from the Cold War. USAMRIID intercepted a partial message about Home Shield routed from someone in the OEM, but it was cut off before anything really useful was transmitted. All we managed to get was the sender's coordinates," Shafer said. He relayed them to me and I repeated them back. "Shouldn't be too hard to find."

"I'll go check it out, sir," I said.

"I appreciate it, son. When you make it here, we'll have a beer and I'll tell you how we ended up here. But there's a fierce looking woman here who wants to talk to you. You have yourself some good luck, and we'll see you soon."

"Dave?" Maya's voice came through the handset before I could reply.

"Hey, baby," I said. My belly felt like I was on a roller coaster ride the second I heard her voice, and I felt my mouth stretch into a smile. "You made it."

"We did. Porsche and Cassie and Bryce are okay, too. Sweet Goddess, I miss you. Are you okay?"

"I'm fine, love," I said. "A little worse for wear, but nothing life threatening. Unless you count teaching Amy to drive." Her laughter fell on my ears like the song of an angel.

"You're braver than I thought," she said. "So, Amy's okay, too?"

"Yeah, she's doing even better than me. Though her vocabulary has gotten a little more…colorful of late. Evidently I'm a terrible father figure that way."

"What *will* they think at the country club? Such a scandal." I laughed and made sure she could hear it. "I don't know where she learns such shitty language."

"No idea. Must be from me. Look, I'm sorry we couldn't go straight to Nate's. I tried to send Amy with the train, I really did. But, unlike her mother, she's a little stubborn."

"It's okay, sweetie. Just get her here safe. Let me talk to her." I handed the handset to Amy with a shake of my head.

"Mom?" she said, suddenly sounding very much her age, and very much like a homesick teenager. I stood and walked to the edge of the roof, looking west at the darkening sky. George came up to stand beside me, and for a moment or two, neither of us spoke.

"I take it you two are going to be moving on," he finally said. I nodded. "It's a shame. You're good in a fight, and after last night, a lot of folks down there think you're some kind of hero." He gestured down at the cathedral below us.

"Believe me, I've got clay feet. In fact, I could use your help with something, if you didn't mind making a bit of a trip."

"Right now, son, you could ask most folks here for just about anything and they'd do it for you. Some of those men and women you-"

"We," I interjected.

"Okay, some of the men and women *we* rescued last night had family here. We owe you and your daughter a lot."

"Wait until you hear the whole story before you go canonizing me," I said before I laid out the quick and dirty version of the situation we had found at the Manson family farm. "I told him I was going to come back and check on the kids in a week or two. Truth is, I never intended to leave those kids there."

"If you were looking for someone to take those children in, you found it," George said. "The only problem you're gonna have is narrowing it down to just one family."

"I need more than that. I need someone to go get them. Someone who will be willing…and someone who *can*…take those kids by force."

"Still think you're gonna have more volunteers than you need, son. I was a coach and a science teacher for twenty years. I know what parents are capable of, both good and bad. Hell, I'll go get those kids myself. Don't you worry. We'll get those children taken care of."

"Then I owe you big time."

"No you don't. It's the right thing to do," he said and put a hand on my shoulder. Amy called out to me and I went back to the radio. In contrast to the smile on her face, her eyes were red and her cheeks were damp.

"Mom wants to talk to you again," she said, ending with a sniffle. I took the handset from her.

"Maya?" I said.

"I'm here, baby," she said. "Nate says we can't talk too much longer. Thank you for keeping Amy safe. You make a good father."

"I make a decent stand-in, yeah," I said. "Maybe someday I'll be a good dad. But the only parenting award I qualify for is 'World's Deadliest Dad,' and I think Nate has me beat on that one. I know we don't have much time left to talk. I love you." The last sentence came out so desperate it hurt, and it sounded awkward in my ears, like I was trying to cram more into those three little words than they could ever hold.

"I love you, Dave Stewart," Maya said, and I could hear the same awkward density in her voice. "You come back to me."

"Not even the zombie apocalypse could stop me." I signed off and shut the radio down, then started breaking the antenna down and stowing everything.

"So, what's the plan?" Amy asked as I finished putting things away. I looked down at the coordinates Colonel Shafer had given me and did some quick math in my head. With one degree of latitude being about sixty nine miles, and figuring we were almost due east of Nate's location, our destination was about four degrees north of us, which made it almost 300 miles away.

"We're heading to South Dakota," I said. I headed for the door to the stairs as I talked, and Amy fell in step beside me.

"South Dakota? Why?" Amy asked, her face scrunching up.

"Do you want the boring answer or the exciting one?"

"Give me the boring one first," she said as we started down the stairs.

"We're going to go find an old Continuity of Government facility that was being used by the Office of Emergency Management, and look for information about something called Project: Home Shield." Once I said it out loud, it sounded slightly less boring than it had in my head.

"That was the boring answer?" Amy laughed behind me. "What's the exciting one?"

"We're going to get vital information that will help save the world...and fight ninjas. Because ninjas make everything more exciting." George and Amy both laughed at that.

"We're not walking all the way, are we?" Amy asked.

I shook my head. "No, we'll have to find a working car or something. Preferably something with four wheel drive. The roads are too iffy."

"Ya'll are thinking too big," George said. He opened the doorway into the cathedral and led us back through the smaller office and classroom area to the kitchen. "Grab something to eat, get some rest, and in the morning, I'll show you two how to get around in this neck of the woods."

"I don't know how to ride a motorcycle," Amy said as we stood in the showroom of Bill's Speed and Sport.

"You'll learn," I said. Beside me, George beamed and handed me a handful of keys that he'd taken from behind the counter.

"I suggest you go with the dirt bikes," he said. "And accessorize."

Chapter 6
On the Road Again...
*~ The quest for freedom, dignity and the rights of man will
never end. ~ William J Brennan, Jr.*

Amy goosed the throttle on her Yamaha and sped down the
straightaway, then downshifted as she came to the curved end of
the dirt track. The little WR250R angled into the curve, and my
arms tensed as she let up on the throttle, then goosed it again for
a split second. The heavily modified bike had dumped her a few
times on the curve, but she pulled out without laying it down and
sped toward us. At the last moment, she grabbed the clutch and
braked, sliding to a dusty stop a few feet away. Clad in the armor
and vest we'd worn out of Kansas City and the helmet she'd put
the two blue Mohawk strips on, she was better protected than she
would be in most bike jackets, and the combat boots and greaves
had protected her from road rash when she'd dumped the bike
before.

"I think I'm ready," she said as she took the helmet off. "I felt
it trying to lay over on the curve, but I kept it under me." Her
smile was infectious, and I had to nod in agreement.

"Yes, padawan, I believe you're ready for the trials." I
grabbed my helmet and put it on, then climbed onto my bike.
Like her bike, mine was decked out with a clear four gallon gas
tank, a tank bag strapped over that, with a small set of saddle
bags on the side, and a matching set up on the tail, with a pair of
saddle bags and a tail rack that held our larger gear like sleeping
bags, tent, clothes, cooking kit and the Spitfire. We had found
the one Amy was riding completely decked out in the speed
shop's work area. Using it as a template, we had raided the
store's accessory section and had put my bike together largely on
the spot. Amy refused to part with her Ruger, and the armory had
been stocked with M16A3s, which were too big to carry in
addition to the Ruger. So I had taken the shoulder stock off the
Mossberg and jury rigged a scabbard for it across the handlebars
of her bike. The Ruger rode in a scabbard behind Amy's right
leg. My M4 was in a similar set up, and my Ruger Takedown
pack was strapped to the Spitfire. I'd donated the Glock to the
folks at St Mark's and went back to an M9 with its ubiquitous

nine millimeter round to supplement my two .45s and their dwindling stock of ammunition. With all of the other gear we were carrying, we were only left with room to carry one ammo can and however many rounds we could stuff into our packs and vests. For food, we had stocked ten First Strike Rations apiece and filled our camelbacks. This was the first time we'd tried the bikes fully loaded, and it looked like Amy had the hang of it, though neither of us would be winning any motocross races.

I started my bike and put it in gear, letting Amy take the lead back to the cathedral. We skirted a group of slow moving infected as we crossed the fairgrounds and hit the road going back north. A handful of minutes later, we were pulling into the parking lot at St. Mark's. To my right, the morning sun was just clearing the tree tops and buildings. George was waiting at the gate, his lean, dark face looking a little forlorn. Behind him, we could see several other people, including Dr. Crews.

"Looks like you two are ready to hit the road," he observed as we went through the gate and into the little courtyard.

"Yeah," I agreed. "We've got a long way to go, and the sooner we get there, the sooner we can make it back to our family."

"Hate to see you two leave," he said. "Seems like I've been saying good-bye too much the past couple of weeks or so."

"Hey, we brought another dozen folks to fill in for us," Amy said. "And it's not like you're never going to hear from us again. You have that other radio like ours and the shortwave." Her smile wavered as she tried to cheer him up, and his seemed to get stronger.

"Maybe that's why it's so hard to see you go," he said. "You brought us so many blessings. And Allie is going to help us keep in touch with you. I'm gonna miss your smile around here, Amy." Her smile brightened a couple of megawatts at that.

"George, I owe you my life, and I won't forget that," I said as I put my hand out. He shook it and smiled.

"We'll keep you in our prayers, Dave," he said. "You two stay safe and look out for each other. And don't you worry. We'll go get those kids." I nodded, and turned to Amy. She stepped past me and put her arms around George in a fierce hug before she went to the gate. Dr. Crews came up to me and pressed a small package into my hand.

"Keep that wound cleaned, and change those bandages daily," she said, her voice a little rough. "I didn't let you rescue me so you could die of gangrene."

"Not on my list of things to do," I told her with a weak smile. I turned away and followed Amy out of the gate.

"You know, I'm getting tired of saying goodbye myself," Amy said as she put her helmet on. I buckled mine on and pulled the shooting goggles down over my eyes.

"Me, too, padawan. Me, too." We started the bikes up and waved before we pulled out onto the street. In my rearview mirror, I could see George lift his hand before he turned back and closed the gate. My thoughts wanted to go back to what might be going on in the cathedral after we left, but necessity forced me to focus on the path ahead. The street we were following, Burlington, took us south until we saw the railroad tracks crossing over the road. We turned right on the street before the road dipped under them and crossed the parking lot, then followed the tracks west, following the same route we'd taken to the armory. But instead of turning north, we kept following the tracks until we ran out of town and found ourselves back on flat prairie. A mile or so out of town the tracks crossed a road, and we followed it south about fifty yards until we hit Grand Army of the Republic Road. According to the map on my tank bag, it took us south of several towns to a road that would take us north across the Platte River.

Sure enough, ten minutes later, we were pointing our front tires north on Prosser Road. It was a little disappointing to leave Grand Army of the Republic Road, but it wasn't like many people would get the reference any more. Nebraska was turning out to be a lot like Kansas, miles and miles of nothing but miles and miles. For half an hour, the most interesting thing in sight was the horizon. It was only when we got close to the Platte that we started seeing trees regularly, and even then they were mostly thin saplings choked with brush. Two houses that looked like they'd been built in the Sixties sat on either side of the road, and we did our best not to look very closely at them as we sped toward the narrow, two-lane bridge. Rusted side railings ran along on either side of us as we crossed the sluggish blue-green waters of the Palatte River, then we found ourselves among trees again. The stench of dead things hit our noses as we passed through the wooded area, then we were on another bridge, this one running across a shallow arm of the river that ran through a low, marshy bed. The terrain relinquished its hold on the trees and brush about a mile later when we crossed over a divided highway that was almost devoid of vehicles, and we were back to the unrelenting flatness and endless, vacant sky. For hours, we did nothing but ride through country that, according to George, had less than one person per square mile.

Around noon, I pulled to a stop near a ranch style house just off the road. A Ford F-150 and a pink Cadillac with a Mary Kay sticker shared space in the front driveway. Neither one had been built before the turn of the century, but both looked like they would have run. I stretched slowly as I got off the bike, suddenly keenly aware that I'd been crouched in the same position for more than three hours. Amy groaned behind me as she discovered the same thing. Something was buzzing in my head as I looked around, some sense of wrongness that I couldn't quite place.

"Are you thinking of gassing up here?" she asked as she eyed the house warily.

"It had crossed my mind, yeah," I said.

"I feel kind of bad just taking their stuff. Do you think we should knock and see if anyone's alive?" My answer was interrupted by a desiccated face slamming against the front window of the house. The front window looked straight out onto the yard, but it looked like the front door faced to the side. It took only a second for me to get the M9 out. Through the glass, I could hear the muted growl of the ghoul as she pressed against the window, her pastel blue skirt and jacket stained with blood. Her fist slammed into the oversized pane and started a long crack in it. She hit it again, and more fissures spread from the center of the break.

"Dave?" Amy asked from beside me.

"Get 'er," I said. Her Browning popped three times, and the ghoul fell back from the broken shards of the window. She dropped the barrel a little and straightened. The sound of glass shifting was the only warning we had before the ghoul leaped through the empty frame. Amy's pistol barked again, this time in counterpoint to mine. The ghoul flopped backward in the air and landed on its ass. For a few seconds, we both watched the window, but she was apparently the only survivor. When nothing jumped out of the window at us,. Amy went forward a couple of steps and put a round through the ghoul's face.

"I'm reloading," she said a few seconds later. She pulled a fresh mag from her vest, dropped the magazine from the butt of her pistol and loaded the fresh one in seconds. "I'm good," she said, and I reloaded as well.

With Amy on watch, I grabbed the siphon and stuck the long end into the truck's tank and filled Amy's bike, then started on mine. The truck's tank petered out about halfway through mine, but the Cadillac had enough to finish the job. Minutes later, we were back on the road. By now, the flat terrain was turning into low hills, but we were still in the deep middle of prairie, where the tallest thing around was a telephone pole. If I hadn't passed a sign saying we'd left Kansas a couple of days earlier, I would have sworn we were still in the same state.

After a couple of hours of driving, I pulled off to the right side of the road and rode to the top of a hill. From there, we could see for miles. I stopped the bike and pulled it up on its center stand before I pulled my pack off.

"Lunch time," I said. We ate in silence, speaking only to trade my corn nuts for her peanut butter and crackers out of our MREs.

"I hope we're past this by the time it gets dark," Amy said after she drained the last of the drink mix from the pouch. The wind left a chill in its wake as it hissed through the grass, and I found myself agreeing with her.

"We should be in the Black Hills before dark. Lots of places to hole up there. But for now, get your sword, time to work on form." She groaned but it didn't slow her down. We worked on strikes and defense for half an hour, concentrating on slow versions of each, gradually working our way to half speed. After that, we worked on footwork and thrusts for another half hour, then took a break to stretch before we got back on the bikes and started on our way again.

An hour later, we came across a sign that said Alliance was fifteen miles ahead. If it warranted a sign, then there were enough people to make plenty of infected. But, the good thing about Nebraska was that near towns, most of the land was criss-crossed by farm roads in neat grids. About three miles from town, we took the first road north that we could. About half a mile down, we found ourselves at the driveway to a farm. Amy pulled up beside me after I came to a stop and looked over at me.

"Looks like we ran out of road," she said with a grin. "What now, oh wise and powerful Jedi Master?"

"We don't need roads, padawan," I said. I turned my front wheel to my left and took off. A few seconds later, I heard the sharp buzz of Amy's bike as she followed. The shocks took most of the bumps out of the ride as we skirted the edges of massive circles of tilled land. Our goal was US 385, which ran north out of Alliance. After about a mile, we hit a dirt track that ran alongside another farm. We followed it until it crossed a northbound road, but that one turned out to be almost as short lived as the one we'd just left. Once again, we went west. Then we hit Nebraska 87, and I followed that north, certain it would take us past the northern edge of Alliance.

Ahead and on the right, something caught my eye, and I slowed to take a closer look. A gray structure sat off the road about fifty yards or so, and behind it I could make out a taller yellow one. Slowly, it took shape and I saw that the gray structure was made out of cars. Then I saw the green sign, and I laughed.

"Carhenge Entrance," it read. I slowed to a stop to take a better look, and Amy pulled up beside me.

"Look, Dave!" she called over the sound of the bike's engine. "We found an ancient archeological site! Carhenge!" I laughed again, this time at her feigned ignorance.

"We must be the first humans in hundreds of hours to even see this spot," I said. "Its raw, untamed beauty and the spectacle of ancient Americana."

"Who knew this trip was going to be so educational?" she said. "I want to check it out!" She gunned her bike and turned off the road. For a moment, I considered telling her we had to keep moving, but I slapped that urge down. Seeing her impulsive and playful was a blessing of its own after the past two weeks, so I pulled in behind her. She was off her bike by the time I got my kickstand down and had the Mossberg slung as she headed toward the main attraction. I followed her as she approached the gray cars, her laughter a bright counterpart to the desolate sound of the wind.

"I wish I had a camera!" she called out to me. I looked over my shoulder at the gift shop, then turned back to her and held up one hand with my index finger up. The shop was closed after mid-September, but the door was no match for the pry bar in my pack. There wasn't a lot inside given the time of year, but I found a box of disposable cameras next to an open carton full of Carhenge key chains and a half empty display of M&Ms. I grabbed two of each along with a couple of brochures for the place and headed back out. I had no idea if we'd ever get any pictures developed, but the idea that we might be able to do that someday was the important part.

"Make yourself pretty or whatever," I said as I got closer. She yanked her helmet off and tried to smooth her hair, but the wind caught it and blew it across her face, and I snapped the first picture while she was busy looking exasperated. The gust died down a moment later and I snapped a better pic of her in front of the monument.

"Oh my God!" she cried out a moment later. "Is that a dinosaur? Dave, you've got to get a picture of that…and those four over there!" She ran over and posed in front of the metal dinosaur like she was running from it, then she went to the four painted cars and threw her arms up. Once I took the picture, she ran over to me and took the camera from my hand, then dragged me over to a metal sculpture of a fish. Getting into the spirit of things, I held the pry bar like a fishing pole and posed as if I was trying to reel it in, trying to look shocked at the same time.

"You have seriously got to shave and get a haircut," she said as she advanced the film. "You're starting to look like a homeless guy."

"I think it makes me look rugged and handsome," I said. "Sort of like Hugh Jackman."

"You look more like the Wolf Man than Wolverine," she replied.

"Come on," I said. "We still have some traveling to do. But here's a souvenir." She took the keychain and brochure, then hugged me.

"Oh, they built this place as a memorial for the artist's dad," she said. A few steps later, she added, "We ought to do something like that for Dad."

"We will," I said. "If you're wanting to do Stonehenge, there's plenty of cars laying around, but it'll take some time."

"Dave, stop," she said, her voice suddenly unsteady. "I'm serious."

"So am I. If you want to do something, we'll do it. No matter how big you want to go. He saved my life, too."

"Thanks," she said. We stowed our gear and got back on the bikes, then got back on the road. We hit the next road that went west, then got on 385 going north. Our route took us past the worst of the traffic, but from a town the size of Alliance, that wasn't much. If anyone had tried to get out of town, it looked like they had clear roads to travel on.

The landscape got more interesting about an hour later when we hit the Pine Ridge area. Trees sprang up ahead though they weren't as thick or tall as I'd expect to find in Missouri. We followed the road as it dipped and curved then slowly climbed again before it leveled out. About a mile in, we saw the first infected wandering down the road. I moved to the left side of the road and the infected moved to intercept me, its movements fast. Ghouls. When I was a few yards away, I swerved right, out of reach. Amy followed suit and came around on my right. More infected started to appear ahead of us, too many to simply avoid.

On impulse I broke left and sped through a gate, with Amy only a few feet behind. The dirt road led down a hill. I risked a look to my right and saw that the infected hit the barbed wire fence at full speed. It held up for a few heartbeats, then broke under their numbers. Then we were among the trees and I lost sight of them. The bikes were a lot faster than even the fastest human, and among trees, they wouldn't be moving in a straight line. If we were lucky, they'd try to follow the sound of the bikes and run off a ridge or break their legs somehow. Luck wasn't something I'd learned to count on, so I kept the bike's throttle wide open. The road turned right up ahead, so I slowed down and leaned into the turn, hoping Amy made it, too. When I straightened out, she pulled up on my left, then sped ahead and broke left again. This time I was the one trying to keep up as she wove through the trees, following a dirt trail that I could barely see.

The trail curved right before it came out of the trees, and Amy gunned the engine on her bike, heading for a dirt road. It turned into asphalt a few hundred yards later, and we sped along it as the first of the infected broke from the trees behind us. They fell behind and out of sight as the road curved. Amy looked back over her shoulder and grinned, then let off on the throttle. Eventually, the road T'ed and we turned back east until we ended up on 385 again. For the next hour or so, we simply rode north, following the highway. We skirted Chadron and crossed the border into South Dakota ten minutes later. About an hour later, I pulled to a stop outside of a town called Hermosa and broke out the Spitfire to check our coordinates.

"We head about ten miles west from here," I said as Amy came back from her trip to answer nature's call. "And maybe two miles north."

"That's right in the middle of the park," she said with a nod toward a sign advertising the shortest route to Mt Rushmore. "Maybe we can stop and see that."

"Sure," I said as I finished strapping the radio back to my bike. "For that matter, if it isn't overrun with infected, we could probably camp nearby. I'm sure there's a campground we can use." We started the bikes up and followed the road west, taking the winding turns as fast as we dared. The signs for Mt Rushmore put it very close to our true destination, and I started to get the strange feeling that it might actually *be* that destination. We blew through a tiny town a mile or so out, leaving a hundred or so second stage infected shambling in our wake, and took the last couple of miles as fast as we dared. Finally, we pulled into the entrance to Mt. Rushmore.

Whatever I had been expecting, it wasn't a nearly empty place. We took the driveway up to the top of the parking garage, and I pulled up short when I saw two Blackhawks parked on the top level. A Chinook rested on the next parking structure.

"I think we're in the right place," I said after I pulled my helmet off. The hackles on the back of my neck started to rise as I looked around, and my gaze was slowly pulled northwest.

"Do you feel that?" Amy said.

"Yeah," I answered. "There's an alpha zombie around here somewhere."

"What the hell is it doing way out here?" she asked.

"No idea," I said as I pulled the M4 from its scabbard. "In Springfield, they thought Patient Zero was the source of the infection, so I figured they'd show up where there were a lot of infected. The only one I know of that wasn't in a big city was the one in Nevada. And DHS imported that one."

"That didn't go well. I hope that isn't going on here."

"Me, too," I said. "But always assume the worst case scenario."

"Yeah, this is gonna be real fun," Amy said as she slung her Ruger and grabbed the Mossberg off the front of her bike's handlebars. I cycled a round into the chamber of the M4 and started toward the entrance to the park itself. Just to the right inside the arched entryway was the bookstore. A guided audio tour booth sat on the opposite side, flanked by the restrooms.

"If you have to go, now's the time to brave the possibly zombie infested bathrooms," I said as we passed them.

"I'm never peeing again," she said. "Thanks, Dave." I looked back over my shoulder at her to flash a grin, and my eyes went to the lettering beneath the bookstore's larger signage. *National Park Service, U.S. Department of the Interior.* Making a mental note to avoid hunting while on Park Service grounds, or at least to not get caught at it, I pressed on under the gaze of the four presidents above the end of the walkway. We made our way down the stone paved walkway, guns at the ready, eyes moving left and right.

"Hold up for a second," Amy said after we passed under the second archway. I looked back at her and saw her snap a picture of the monument. "Might as well get one while things are calm, right?" she asked.

I shook my head. "Might as well, gift shop's closed." We followed the pathway through a series of columns bearing state flags, then found ourselves looking over the amphitheater. I stopped while Amy took another picture, and concentrated on the prickly feeling that was running down my spine. Again, I let my gaze follow that feeling, and found myself looking at the cliff face. Though my eyes naturally wanted to look at the massive faces looking down at me, somehow, I was sure that what I wanted to kill was below them and behind them. I went over to one of the maps posted near the edge of the amphitheater and looked at the route of the Presidential Trail.

"Are we on the wrong side of the mountain?" Amy asked.

"Maybe," I said. "Let's follow the trail here and see if we can get closer." The first part of the trail felt like we were moving away from it, but when it curved around, it started getting stronger again. As we got to a curve that started to head back across the front of the sculpture, I heard something moving in the brush above us. I froze and pointed to one of the trees nearby, leading by example as I took cover behind another tree. Whoever it was, they were a good distance away, and their bushcraft was for crap. I could hear rocks tumbling down beneath them and small twigs snapping under their feet. Either they weren't trying to be stealthy, or they were failing miserably at it.

I moved to Amy's side and pointed to a boulder on her right, then held a finger to my lips before nodding toward where I wanted her to go. She nodded back to me and padded to the boulder. I followed once she got there, then headed past her to a nearby tree. Amy followed when I gestured for her to, and we leapfrogged like that another few yards up the trail. I motioned for her to take her helmet off and duck down behind a boulder, then we waited as the group of people got closer. Before long, they came into view.

For all that they weren't stealthy, these men knew their business. They covered each other as they made their way down to our position, their eyes on their flanks and rear as much as on what was in front of them. Not a one of them looked like he was under two hundred pounds, and not a one of them was dressed for the woods. I counted eight men in slacks and bullet proof vests over long sleeved button down shirts. They carried FN P90s like they knew how to use them, and I pitied anyone they were serious about killing. I'd seen hard men before; Nate was a former Delta operator, and Captain Adams' Special Forces team was concentrated badass, and these men had the same look about them. The only thing that was keeping me safe just now was the fact that I knew how to hide and move quietly in the woods better than they did. Most of that skill was in knowing where to step, how to stay still and how to break up your body's silhouette. I let them get past us before I moved to a tree behind them and crouched down again.

"Gentlemen," I said aloud. Anything else I planned to say was drowned out in a hail of gunfire.

"Contact rear!" someone called out.

"Ya think!" I yelled. "God damn it! I'm not trying to hurt you!"

"We know there's two of you," another man yelled. "Both of you step out where we can see you!"

"Who are you?" I asked.

"None of your business. Now step out or we'll open fire again!"

"That isn't very reassuring," I said. There was a long silence, then I heard one of the men speaking softly.

"We're with the government," the guy who had been doing the talking said. "We're not going to hurt you." It was still a risk, but I had a hunch about these men. I stood and held the M4 by the barrel, then held it out where they could see it. I moved out from behind the tree behind it, and found myself facing eight gun barrels.

"Well, you didn't shoot me on sight, so that's a good start," I said.

"Where's your friend?" the lead man demanded.

"My daughter is nearby," I said. The man closest to the talker looked over at him, and I could see doubt cross the faces of the others. The leader looked to the guy next to him and nodded toward me, then lowered his own gun.

"Stand down," he said. The others lowered their weapons, except for the one beside him. His gun stayed on me.

"Amy, hold your shotgun by the barrel and hold it away from your body, then stand up where these men can see you," I said. The leader started when Amy stood up less than ten feet from him.

"There's someone who wants to see you," the leader said. "We're going to have to ask you to disarm first, though." Beside him, Amy made a disgusted noise. "Sorry, miss, that's not a request."

"I wasn't saying no," she said. "It's just that...disarming is kind of a long process." She handed one of them her shotgun and started drawing weapons slowly. I stepped forward and started the process myself, chuckling as the man who was taking my weapons started having to hand things off to make room. Four pistols, three knives, two rifles and a sword later, I was as disarmed as I was going to get barring a cavity search. Amy stepped up beside me looking decidedly unhappy about the current state of affairs.

"If you'll please follow us," the leader said. The path back up the hill turned into a set of wooden steps that led to a gap behind the sculptures, and then to an opening in the cliff wall. They led us to the back of a narrow cave where a thick door stood open. Through that was a hallway that led to a set of metal stairs. With every step we took, the prickling feeling got stronger. Finally, we came to an open room with a long table set in the middle. An old base relief map covered its surface, and framed versions of various documents adorned the walls. A woman with graying black hair in a rumpled pair of coveralls stood near the head of the table, flanked by another man and a woman, both looking like they'd been dressed by the same person who had dressed the men escorting us. The woman in the coveralls looked older then the others around her, and she was the only person in the room who wasn't armed. She stepped forward and extended a hand to me.

"I'm Madeline Morris," she said, her voice a strong but pleasant contralto. "I'm sorry for the rather hostile reception you got outside. I'm sure you have a lot of questions, starting with what this place is, and who we are."

"No, ma'am," I said as I shook her hand. "That part I'm pretty sure of. This is a Cold War era continuity of government bunker. And, it's nice to meet you Madam President."

Chapter 7
Theories & Revelations
~ People love conspiracy theories. ~ Neil Armstrong

"How do you know that?" President Morris demanded as ten gun barrels zeroed in on me.

"It's kind of obvious," I said, secretly pleased with myself. Okay, maybe not so secretly pleased, but no one was asking and I wasn't telling. "I mean, you're in a secret government bunker, surrounded by athletic looking young men and women armed with FN P90s. They're either with the Secret Service or Stargate Command. Since the SGC isn't real, I'm going with Secret Service. And who else would be holed up in a secret COG bunker with a detail of Secret Service agents? So, where were you on the line of succession?"

"Secretary of the Interior. You're remarkably well informed, Mister...?" Morris left the question hanging. Something about the way she asked it made me wonder if she really needed me to give her the answer.

"Stewart," I said. "My name's Dave Stewart."

"Did you by chance write Operation: Terror?" Morris asked.

"Yeah," I said with a smile. "And the Frankenstein Code. You've read my books?"

"Not by choice," she said. "My predecessor's analysts describe your work as juvenile, needlessly violent and written at a fifth grade reading level. They also wanted you detained indefinitely for treason."

"Oh," I said as my ego deflated. Talk about tough critics.

"Damn, do you need some ice for that burn?" Amy asked with a mocking wince.

"My predecessor's analysts were idiots," she went on. "They had a tendency to see enemies where there were none. Fortunately, the President was smart enough to know when not to listen to them."

"The President even knew who I was?" I said. "I'm not sure I *want* to know what he thought."

"He thought your books were harmless enough," she said with a small smile. "But, your writing career aside, how did you know I was here?"

"I didn't," I said. "I was just asked to pick up some info at an old COG base about Operation: Home Shield."

"By whom?"

"Colonel Schafer, with US SOCOM," I said. Morris frowned and tilted her head.

"And you talked to him recently?" she asked.

"Last night."

"Come with me," she said after a moment, then turned and headed through a door behind her. I followed her into what looked like a command center. The wall to my left was covered with maps pinned to bulletin boards, while the right side of the room was occupied by a bank of radios, some of them antiques and some copies of the Spitfire I'd left on my bike. In the center of the room was a table with four people at laptops, two to a side. Every eye turned to us when we came in, and one of the people at the table stood and approached us.

"Ma'am, Special Agent Shepherd has the intru-" she stopped abruptly when she caught site of Amy and me. "The bikes are in the garage, ma'am."

"Good, Simone. Reactivate Colonel Schafer's file. Mr. Stewart tells me he's alive."

"Madam President, with all due respect," Simone said with a sidelong glance at me, "FOB Oscar was a total loss. Sikes left the soldiers there to die."

"I helped Schafer get out along with Captain Adams' team."

Simone turned to Morris. "Is he really..?" She nodded, and Simone turned back to me with a speculative look. "You've been declared dead twice. Between you and Carson, it's like Whack-a-Mole. Okay, we'll reactivate Schafer and Karma One."

"President Morris," I said, "before we go any further, I have to ask you something. Where is the alpha zombie?" The room went quiet, and again, every eye focused on us.

"Mister Stewart, there are no zombies here," Morris said smoothly.

"Bullshit," Amy said. "We can feel it." That got a few gasps. Morris looked at Amy and stepped up to her.

"What do you mean you can feel it?" she asked in a voice that even Amy backed down from.

"Amy and I can both tell when there are zombies around," I interjected. "Especially the alpha zombies, the ones the CDC labeled Patient Zeros. Tends to make us a little cranky." Morris's face hardened as I spoke, and her eyes narrowed.

"Mr. Stewart, you seem to know an awful lot about these zombies. Far more, in fact, than you ought to."

"Of course I know a lot about them!" I said. "I've killed enough of them. And not just your run of the mill stage one and stage two cases. We've killed some infected that would make you lose your lunch. You think there are just three kinds? Hell no. There are Screamers, Burners, Blobs and last but certainly not least, there are the Trolls."

"Ogres," Amy said.

"Whatever. The point is we've been out there for the past two weeks fighting them. We *know* our infected, maybe better than you do. We can feel them, and we can kill them like nobody's business. And we can both feel the alpha zombie you have locked away in here."

"If there was an…alpha zombie in here, you wouldn't be cleared to know about it," Morris said. "Furthermore, if you did have that kind of-" she stopped as the door on the other side of the room opened and a woman in a lab coat burst into the room.

"Madam President, she's awake," the woman said. Her gaze fell on us before she continued "And she's talking."

"McGregor," Morris said crisply, "Take these two to the dining room and keep an eye on them. Phillips, Trowbridge, you're with me." She followed the doctor and McGregor, an older looking agent with a little silver in his close cropped black hair, led us out the same door his boss had exited through, but instead of turning left in her footsteps, he led us to the right, past two more hallways until we came to a set of double doors that led into an old cafeteria. He pointed to a round table that was surrounded by orange and green plastic chairs. Amy and I sat. Most of the lights were off, save for those over the door and in the kitchen area, leaving the room dimly lit except for a couple of pools of light.

"Did we miss lunch?" Amy asked after a couple of minutes. McGregor nodded and made an affirmative sounding noise. She rolled her eyes and shook her head, then leaned back in her chair.

"So, how did this lady end up president?" she asked after a few moments.

"She's further up the line of succession than Shaw," I said. "Homeland Security is the newest addition to the chain, so the Secretary of pretty much anything else would outrank him. Or, in this case, the Secretary of Everything Else."

"You lost me," she said.

"It's something my granddad used to say. He was a Forest Ranger for a few years, and he used to joke that he worked for the Department of Everything Else, because the Department of the Interior covered so many things." Seconds later, the doctor poked her head in.

"Come with me," she said. We got up and followed, wondering if someone had started rationing words or something. The doctor type led us back down the hallway, past several doors until we came to one on the right marked "Infirmary." With every step we took, the feel at the back of my head got stronger, until my heart was pounding in my chest and my fists were clenched at my sides. By the time she pushed the door open, I was ready to rip someone's head off.

The first thing I saw was the alpha zombie, or what was left of it. Its legs and arms had been removed just above the elbows and knees. Before death, she had been blonde, and her face and hair seemed very well preserved by comparison to the rest of her. She was still gaunt and pale, but she didn't have the desiccated, slightly rotted look the last alpha I'd seen had. They had her in a metal box that had a clear cover on it with holes drilled in it. Her display case was tilted so that it was almost upright, giving her a view of the room, and vice versa.

"So, are these the people you were talking about?" Morris asked. The corpse in the box looked at us and nodded, her face splitting into a sickly sweet smile.

"Yes, the Nephilim!" the alpha cooed. She let out a giggle that sent ice cold claws down my spine. "Thank you, Maddie."

"Why did you want to see them?" Morris asked.

"Because the closer they are to me, the stronger I get. In a few minutes, I'll be able to get out of this box and kill every last one of you." She looked expectantly at the Secret Service members in the room, then shook her head. "Well, aren't you going to kill them? It's the only way to stop me." Morris shook her head.

"No, Sarah, we're not. I kept my end of the bargain. It's time for you to keep yours. Tell me what you know about them."

"Well, the scruffy looking little primate is the Survivor. He's been a bad little monkey. The little girl with him...she's his apprentice, his protégé if you will. We haven't decided what to call her yet." Beside me, Amy bristled, but she kept her mouth shut when I put an arm out in front of her.

"Were they in Springfield?" Morris asked pointedly.

"The Survivor was," zombie Sarah said with a pout. "He hurt poor Deacon."

"What about Kansas City?"

"Oh, they were both in Kansas City. They killed so many of the Necromancer's children. He's quite the artist, you know. Such a waste. Are you sure you won't shoot just one of them for me?"

"Are there other kinds of infected?" Morris asked.

"Oh yes, Maddie," the alpha said. "More than we could ever hope for. Even at our height, we never dreamed that we had such potential. The sad thing is, you pathetic little monkeys perfected the Asura *by mistake!*" The last two words turned into a bitter sounding bark.

"What do you mean?" Morris demanded, her face a little pale now.

"I mean you awakened the Asura, Maddie," the dead woman said, her voice low and frosty, "Something that your ancestors never wanted to see the light of day again. You woke it up, and then you started trying to tamper with it. You tried to tame something bigger than you, and you forgot that sometimes the unknown is hidden for a reason. And now...now we're killing you. We're killing you better than we ever did before, and you made it all possible."

"I've heard enough," Morris said. "Dr. Parsons, put her back in the box." Parsons, the woman who had brought us, nodded and went to the gurney that supported Sarah. Morris gestured for us to follow her and went across the hall to an office. She led us past the outer room to a second office, this one with a faded Presidential Seal painted on the wall behind the broad, wood desk. A carpet had been laid out on the concrete floor and some fairly new couches and chairs had been moved in, but none of them seemed to belong, either in the room or with each other. She motioned to a pair of chairs, then moved to the love seat. As she sat, she pulled an ashtray from the center of the old wooden coffee table toward her and reached into the right breast pocket of her coveralls to retrieve a pack of cigarettes and a lighter.

"Madam President," I started, but she waved me to silence as she lit up and took a deep drag.

"Ugh," she muttered. "I'm down to menthols. I should have started with those. But I guess this will make it easier to quit." The smoke went almost straight up and disappeared into one of the vents overhead, which kept the worst of the smoke from Amy and me. After a couple more puffs, she turned to us. "Please, Mr. Stewart, call me Madeline, or Miss Morris if you have to be formal."

"So, where did you dig her up?" Amy asked, pointing back toward the door with her thumb.

"Washington," Morris said. "Her name is…*was* Sarah Bach. She was a state representative in Texas. Before she turned into *that*, she was one of the most decent human beings I'd ever met. Raised her kids on her own after her husband died in Iraq in '04, got her real estate license, started her own business, even sang in her church choir. The sad thing is, I don't even know why she was in Washington when the outbreak started. But I'm curious. You weren't surprised when she called you Nephilim. I take it you've been called that before."

"The alpha zombie in Kansas City said it was one of many names that 'people like me' had been called through the years. But Nephilim are supposed to be the offspring of fallen angels who married human women."

"Genesis 6:4," Morris said somberly. "The Nephilim were in the Earth in those days, and also after that, when the sons of God came in unto the daughters of men, and they bore children to them; the same were the mighty men that were of old, the men of renown."

"My parents were hardly fallen angels, and I'm not exactly mighty," I said.

"But you can tell when alpha zombies are nearby. And I think people like you scare them a little. I definitely want Dr. Parsons to take some blood samples from you."

"Great," Amy muttered. "More needles."

"Someone else has taken blood samples?" Morris asked.

"A doctor we know who was researching the Asura virus," I said. "So, Mad-...Miss Morris, why trust us now?" I asked, wanting to change the subject.

"Because until ten minutes ago we were completely out of our depth. Do you know how many people I have working for me, aside from the fifteen people you saw when you arrived? None. I'm the president of a little bunker with a staff of ten Secret Service members, four analysts from Air Force One and one person with a doctorate in virology. That's why I haven't declared myself. Shaw would stop at nothing to kill me if he knew I was still alive."

"What's changed?" I asked. She took one last drag off her cigarette and crushed it out in the ashtray, then walked around to the desk and opened a drawer. When she came back, she was carrying a thick folder that was covered in red classification stamps. The lowest one I could see was Top Secret.

"More than you could imagine," she said as she laid the folder down in front of me. "This was the information Col. Schafer sent you for. Project: Home Shield. A plan to help reclaim the United States should the Asura outbreak come to pass. It made use of evac plans to safe zones, Special Forces teams inserted to help pockets of survivors create their own safe zones, seaborne resources, you name it. Even this bunker is a part of it."

"Why show me this? This shit's so classified that even if you ARE cleared for it, you probably aren't cleared for it."

"Because, Mr. Stewart, your books were the pebble that started this avalanche." She smiled as I gaped at her.

"You've got to be kidding me," I said.

"I wish I was, but the truth is, if it wasn't for the books Reid had you write, no one outside of SOCOM would have known about the threat the Asura virus posed. Or the threat Monos posed. When Reid went public through you, he set off a shitstorm in Washington. The Department of Defense and the entire intelligence community wanted him to suffer an unfortunate accident. Once word of that got back to the White House, the President started a quiet investigation, and from that, Home Shield was born."

"Okay, you're welcome, I guess," I said. "I'm glad I'm not the only one who thinks Monos had something to do with this."

"They certainly knew this was coming. We believe Dr. Lennox drew the right conclusion in Iraq, that the people who confiscated the Asura samples and his research were from Monos. We suspected that they knew this was going to happen, but we didn't know how. Sarah's little speech in there about tampering with it makes me wonder if…" She let the sentence trail off, her face stricken.

"If Monos set it loose on purpose?" I supplied.

"I doubt that," she said with a shake of her head. "There is no return on it. I don't know exactly what Monos' role in all of this is, but I'm fairly certain that they didn't intend to unleash a zombie apocalypse."

"But that still doesn't explain what changed today."

"Until you showed up, I thought the Project was completely off line, and that all of its assets were compromised. Shaw has been trying to claim control over any Special Operations assets he can, but shortly after Springfield fell, all the special operations teams went dark. The regular military hasn't been much more cooperative, aside from a few units that the DHS already had some operational control over, like the drone pilots out of March Air Force Base. The problem is, sometimes we don't know if a unit's been destroyed or if they're just not responding. Sarah just confirmed almost everything you told me, and gave us a lot more than she thinks."

"So, you think the spec ops teams went dark because they don't know who to trust," I said. "Let's say you *can* get Schafer on board, then what?"

"Then we activate whatever's left of Home Shield and start trying to save as many people as we can. Beyond that, you're not cleared to know." Her shoulders slumped as she said it and her head drooped.

"So, you want me to do what?" I asked. "Call Schafer and tell him to put the word out to the good guys that you're the real deal or something?"

"Something like that," she said. "Contact the colonel, and let me handle the rest."

"Yes, ma'am," I said, letting a little sarcasm creep into my voice. "But you're gonna have to wait a little bit. My next scheduled check in isn't until later tonight."

"I've waited this long, I can wait a few more hours. In the meantime, you might as well take a shower and get something to eat. Agent McGregor will show you where everything is."

"Thank you, ma'am," I said as I got to my feet.

"Before you go," Morris said as she picked up the file, "You were a sergeant when you got out of the service, right?"

"Staff sergeant, yes ma'am."

"Thank you, that's all for now. Let McGregor know when you need to contact Col. Schafer." Our Secret Service agent led us to a dorm with separate men's and women's showers.

"This place was stocked with stuff from the seventies," he said as he pointed to a table stacked with towels, toiletries and clothes. "We found some better stuff, though." Amy and I helped each other out of our armor, then went to the table. The towels and wash cloths bore the name of a nearby hotel, and some of the shirts bore the Mt Rushmore image on them and still had price tags from the park's gift shop. The pants were mostly the dark green of Park Ranger uniforms, though a few pairs of jeans had made it into the mix as well. I grabbed a fresh t-shirt and pants, the broke into a package of fresh briefs that looked like they were about my size before I grabbed a towel and loaded it down with stuff for the shower.

Standing under the stream of hot water washed away what felt like years of wear and a semi-permanent feeling of grime. The last time I'd been able to take a shower had been the day everything had gone to shit. I'd availed myself of sponge baths at Heartland, but beyond that, swimming across the Kansas River was the closest to actual bathing I'd come since the start of the zombie apocalypse. At first, all I could do was stand under the shower head and let the hot water run down my skin. But, after a couple of luxurious minutes of that, I doused my head with shampoo and took the repeat option on that before I scrubbed myself down twice, being careful of my new battle wound . Once the water started to cool down, I reluctantly got out and toweled myself off.

Finally, I faced myself in the mirror, and found myself forced to do something that grated on my adult sensibilities: agree with a teenager. Amy was right, I definitely needed a shave and a haircut. My hair was just brushing my shoulders, and my beard had gone beyond stubble and was just starting to get past the unkempt stage on me. At the moment, only one of those could be taken care of. I debated keeping the beard, but I figured there would be plenty of time to grow it out later. Without clippers, it took twice as long with the cheap disposable razor to scrape my face smooth but the result was worth the minor nick. With my jawline and chin once more exposed to the world, I stepped out looking and feeling like a new man. Amy was waiting for me by the table, wearing Ranger uniform pants and a Mt Rushmore t-shirt with a red, white and blue design on it. I'd opted for the larger blue shirt.

"Dinner's in a few minutes," McGregor said with a pointed glance at his watch. Not needing to be told twice, we slipped on a pair of souvenir flip-flops and followed him back down to the cafeteria, which was now brighter and more occupied, even if it wasn't close to full. Covered pans filled a small buffet line and there were small pizzas under a warming lamp next to it.

"How much are we allowed to get?" I asked as Amy and I grabbed plates.

"As much as you want," McGregor said.

"Aren't you rationing this?" Amy asked.

"Rationing?" McGregor laughed. "We can't eat this fast enough. All of this is from the restaurant up top, and they average about five thousand people or so a day through the park. We're trying to go through it before it goes bad."

"What about after?" Amy asked, mirroring my own concern.

"This place has enough supplies to keep three hundred people fed for five years," McGregor said as he ladled something thick and brown into a bowl. The aroma hit my nostrils like a brick, and my mouth watered. Since rationing wasn't a concern at the moment, I grabbed a bowl and a plate and hit the buffet like a linebacker. Amy did almost as much damage as I did, but I figured she was just pacing herself. Once I made it to the table, I started with a slice of pizza, and while it should have tasted a little bland, my tastebuds were in heaven.

"I've been craving pizza since all this started," I mumbled around my third bite. Across the table from me, Amy was half way through a bottle of Sprite, her eyes closed as she savored the taste of sugary lemon lime soda.

"I'm taking like a case of this with me," she said after she lowered the bottle.

"You two act like you haven't seen real food for weeks," one of the analysts said to me.

"MREs and camp food," Amy said as she grabbed a slice of pizza of her own and bit into it. "The last real meal we had was the beef stew Mom cooked at Sherwood."

"Well, we had the meatloaf when we were at Nevada," I said.

"That was like, Marine food," Amy countered through a bite of pizza. "Totally doesn't count."

"What about the meals at Heartland?" I asked. She shook her head quickly. "You're right. Camp food."

"Dorm food," she countered. "But that fried chicken the other day was pretty damn good."

"Except for the bowl of psycho we had for dessert," I said. We both grimaced and nodded at that. After that, an uncomfortable silence fell for a few moments. We managed to ignore it by eating like starved refugees. Finally, Simone took a quick breath and opened her mouth.

"So, you two have been on the move since Z Monday?" she asked.

"Pretty much," Amy said.

"What's it like out there?" the analyst next to me asked. We paused for a few moments, and the look on Amy's face told me she was as unsure of how to answer that as I was.

"It's fucked up out there," another Secret Service agent said from further down the table. "You don't have to ask *them* to know that." He stopped to shovel another forkful of food into his mouth from the stack on his plate before he spoke again. "Ask our damn pilots, or the agents we had to put down out there what it's like. They're nothing special. All they are is a couple of civilians." All eyes turned toward him and he shrugged. "What? I'm just being honest."

"You're being a dick, Landry," Simone said. She turned to us and lowered her voice "Don't mind him. Living underground turned him into a troll." Amy managed a brave attempt at a smile and nodded. We ate in silence after that, and I watched as Landry got up a few minutes later.

Something about the man bugged the hell out of me, but I couldn't put my finger on it. I followed him with my eyes as he went behind the counter and set his plate in the rack on the commercial grade dishwasher. On his way back up front, he opened a glass fronted refrigerator and pulled out a clear plastic container and a bottle of cola, then stopped to grab a couple of bags of chips before he came back around front. He was big, like most of the Secret Service agents, with a standard DC buzz cut in issue brown. Brown eyes lingered on Amy for a moment, then he crossed behind me. His left arm slid between the analyst and me a moment later, and he leaned in close to her.

"The invitation's still open, Danielle," he said softly enough that almost everyone could hear. "Best offer you're gonna get."

"Answer's still fuck off," Danielle said, her tone actually pitched low enough that I could barely hear it. "And that's the best *you're* gonna get." Landry shoved the table a couple of inches forward as he straightened, then stalked off without another word. As he left, I noticed Amy's head turning to follow him as well.

"Asshole," Amy said as the doors swung closed behind him.

"You have no idea," Simone said. "It never goes much beyond a little posing and a few crude jokes, though. He's mostly just a harmless jerk." By then, I'd made my way through everything on my plate. I hadn't even left the crust of the pizza. I took my plate in the back and set it in the same rack Landry had, then stopped to grab a package of mixed fruit and another soda.

"I'm gonna go rack out for a little while," I said to McGregor. "Is there an alarm clock or something I can use to make sure I'm up by midnight?"

"I'll make sure you're up," Simone said. "Maddie wants to be there when you make the call anyway." I nodded and stumbled for the door. Really full for the first time in a couple of days, my body reminded me I had been on a motorbike for most of the day. I made it to the barracks room and kicked the flip-flops under one of the bunks and crawled under the wool blanket. The bed was the softest thing I'd ever felt, except maybe for the pillow under my face.

I took a deep breath and let my body settle into the mattress. Seconds later, something grabbed my shoulder and I came up off the bed. My feet got caught up in something and I hit the floor hard. When my hand hit my waist and didn't find a knife, I didn't waste time looking for it. Instead, I scrambled to my feet and looked for my attacker. Sudden light blinded me, and I heard voices nearby.

"What is it?"

"Whass goin' on?"

"Damn it kill that light!"

Simone was climbing to her feet next to the bunk I'd been on, and Amy was up and blinking to my right. Slowly my wits settled about my brainpan, and I understood what had happened.

"Sorry," I said as I straightened up from a crouch. "My bad." Grumbles came from behind me as the lights were shut off again, and Simone walked toward me rubbing her shoulder.

"That's one mean punch," she said. "A few inches higher and I might have needed some new dental work."

"You're lucky he didn't have a knife," Amy said as she sat back down on her bunk and started lacing her shoes on.

"Your file didn't mention PTSD," Simone said as I walked past her and grabbed my flip-flops.

"I wasn't diagnosed with it," I told her as I headed for the door. "I spent most of my time in Iraq in the Green Zone, and I never saw actual combat. Hell, I only went outside the bubble twice."

"As opposed to spending the last two and a half weeks in zombie infested territory," Morris said from the door. "We should have anticipated some side effects from that."

"No worries," I said with a casual wave of my hand. "It's my first zombie apocalypse, too. No one expects you to know it all coming out of the gate." The hallway was dimly lit, but when we stepped into the situation room, all of the lights were still on. Simone gestured me toward the radios on the far wall. Theirs was the newer Shadowfire version of the AN/PSC5, but the basics were still the same.

"This is Magic Man, calling Jayhawk," I said.

"Jayhawk here," Nate's voice came back almost immediately. "You just cost me a million dollars."

"Told you betting against me was a bad plan," I said. "Is Schafer around?"

"Yeah, he's been breathing down my neck all damn night. One second."

"This is Col. Schafer," I heard a moment later. "Did you find the info on Home Shield?"

"Yeah, about that," I said with a grin. "We stopped by, took a few pictures of Mt. Rushmore, even grabbed a few souvenirs from their shop, got a bite to eat in the diner, and you'll never guess who we bumped into."

"Spare me the bullshit, Stewart," Schafer snapped. "What did you find?"

"Well, I was trying to ease you into it, but if you insist," I said as I looked over my shoulder. "Hold for the President." I stood up and let Morris have the seat. Almost immediately, Simone pulled me toward the exit.

"What are you doing?" I demanded.

"A lot of her conversation with the colonel is going to be classified."

"She let us see the Home Shield file," I said as we stepped into the hallway, "but her talking to Schafer is above my pay grade?"

"You had a need to know," Simone said as the door closed behind us. "Now you don't. Besides, you already knew about Home Shield. If it's any consolation, I have to stay out here for this part, too." We cooled our heels in the hallway for a few minutes. When the door opened, Morris' looked like a weight had been lifted from her shoulders, and the beginnings of a smile were starting to crack the unexplored regions of her cheeks. We followed her into the room and she signaled to Simone, who turned and locked the door. When the tumbler clicked into place, Morris picked up the microphone and keyed it.

"Colonel, would you confirm for Mr. Stewart that he is to bring me to your location, please?"

"Yes, ma'am," Schafer's voice came over the speakers. "Dave, over Nate's protests, I've agreed to have the president brought here. Her location might be compromised, so we need you to guide her here."

"And you thought *you* had a big target on your back," Amy said.

"Not helping," I muttered to her. "Understood, colonel. I'll get her there."

"Good man. Madam President, in light of our previous conversation, I suggest reactivating Mr. Stewart's enlistment."

"Agreed," Morris said, and this time the smile began to spread.

"Wait a second," I said. "I finished my mandatory eight more than a year ago. I am not about to let you shanghai me into this."

"Only the Navy shanghaies people, son," Schafer said. "You're being drafted."

From the Journal of Maya Weiss
November 2, 2013

I got to see a rare thing today: Nate Reid impressed with something. We had parked the two convoys on the other side of the tree line, and Nate hadn't made it down to see what he'd been roped into until this morning. We had stayed at his cabin that first night, and when we came back down the next morning, two tent cities had cropped up overnight. On one side, there was the military camp. Straight rows of tents with a group of bigger tents for supplies, eating and admin. Someone had even set up a flag pole. The Heartland camp was on the other side, and it was just as orderly. Half of the tents were the kind you'd get from any sporting goods store, but the other half...it was like stepping into history. Medieval style tents and pavilions were set up in neat rows, with a larger pavilion at one end surrounded by smaller tents.

On its own, that was pretty cool, but then we got to the "parking lot" at the far end. Dozens of trucks, vans and buses were parked next to the line of military trucks, and they were in the middle of unloading them when we walked up. It wasn't until I saw the stuff piled up at the end of the row that I really got the scope of what the Heartland people had done. Lumber, drywall, bags of concrete, portable buildings, generators and boxes of tools were waiting to be put to use, and one of the Heartlanders told us it was going to take about two days to finish unloading everything. Nate just stood there for a moment and stared.

Dr. Shaked and Pete Gill had planned for the Heartland project to house three hundred people and feed them for almost a year. And they did it in less than two weeks, with a lot of help. Nate wasn't the only person who was impressed.

One thing is certain: We're all going to be very busy.

Chapter 8
Out of the Eagle's Nest
*~ Security is mostly a superstition. It does not exist in nature,
nor do the children of men as a whole experience it. Avoiding
danger is no safer in the long run than outright exposure. Life is
either a daring adventure, or nothing. ~*
Helen Keller

"We call it Stagecoach," McGregor said as we loaded our
gear onto the armored vehicle. "It's built off the M117
Guardian." The big vehicle in front of us looked a lot like the
convoy security escorts I'd seen in Iraq. Its sides were angled to
keep from presenting a flat surface to RPG or IED blasts, and it
sat on four thick tires that came up to my chest. An easy eight
feet high and more than twenty feet long, it sported a low turret
with twin barrels that pointed toward the ceiling. And, it came in
black. Six of them were lined up in the massive garage area,
alongside a heavy black bus and three olive drab cargo trucks.
People were loading gear and supplies into the Guardian in front
of us and one of the trucks a little ways down. After spending the
morning being poked and tested by Dr. Parsons and the
afternoon learning to use the P90 and the Five-seveN pistol
under McGregor's critical eye, it felt good to be in a little less
structured environment.

"Looks pretty safe," I said as I stroked my chin, "but does it
come with power windows?" McGregor shook his head as he
opened the hatch on the side. The top half swung toward the rear,
and the bottom half folded out to become a step.

"No, but it's fully climate controlled, NBC sealed and the
interior is upholstered in rich, Corinthian naugahyde," he said
with a straight face. "Stow your packs on the top there; long
arms in the racks, side arms on your person, condition three." He
tossed his pack onto the vehicle's roof by example, then climbed
in. I threw mine up alongside his before I unslung the P90 I'd
just been issued and my M4.

"What's condition three?" Amy asked as she tossed hers up
onto the rear deck.

"It means you have a full magazine, but no round in the
chamber and the hammer down," I said.

"We always do that," she said, as if someone had just tried to teach her how to breathe for the first time. "It's that Israel thing you told me about when you first taught me to shoot."

"Israeli carry," I said with a note of pride in my voice that she'd remembered it at all. "Not everyone does it that way all the time. And not all pistols have an open hammer." I stuck my head inside, and let out a low whistle at the size of the interior. The Guardians I remembered from Iraq could only comfortably handle one passenger, but this one sported four seats around the interior, in addition to the three crew positions.

"The Presidential armored car comes in the stretch version," McGregor said as I handed him my M4.

"Too bad we're only taking two of these," I said as I climbed in. "This would make the morning commute a breeze." Amy got in behind me and craned her neck to look around once she handed her Ruger over.

"Do we just sit where we want, or is there assigned seating?" she asked as she folded down one of the black seats.

"Well, the sergeant here is going to be spending a little time in Stagecoach One, so I'd suggest not getting too comfortable."

"Aside from an RTO, what is she going to need me for? Comic relief?" I asked.

"No," McGregor said without a hint of a sense of humor. "Now that you're trained on the P90 and the Five-seveN, you'll be pulling security detail in the vehicle like the rest of us. You'll also get a crash course in driving one of these bad boys, and in operating the turret guns." I stood in the turret and looked at the controls, then ducked back down.

"I'm more management material," I said. "How about vehicle commander? That has a nice ring to it." Once again, my humor bounced off his exterior.

"I'll ask President Morris if she wants comic relief, but I don't think we have any clown makeup." He stepped out and gestured for me to follow him. "One last thing. If something gets in with you, you do not discharge a weapon inside the vehicle. You take a bullet or a bite before you fire at someone inside Stagecoach, you got that?"

"I got it," I said as I caught up with him. "I want to show Amy how to use the P90 before we head out. She needs to know this as much as I do, even if you're not going to issue one to her." His eyes narrowed as he looked over his shoulder at her, then he gave me a steady look.

"Fine, you can *show* her, nothing more," he finally said." She doesn't touch anything, she doesn't fire it. She does not get one issued to her. You will not let her touch one unless she is the last person standing." We followed him toward the side door of the underground garage to get ready for the evening meal.

My M9 had been given to Amy to make room for one of the FN Five-seveN pistols. I still had the Ruger pack for the Takedown, and I had topped off its supplies. As much as I disliked not having it on me or in arm's reach, I left it on my bunk as we headed down to the dining room.

"Airman, you're out of uniform," one of the Secret Service detail said to me.

"Screw you, Armstrong," I said as I sat down across from him. "I'm off duty." That got a laugh from him and everyone else at the table. I looked down at the unadorned Park Ranger uniform I had on. Of all the supplies at Eagle's Nest, the one thing that hadn't been updated since the Fifties had been the wardrobe.

"Why the hell are you even trying?" Landry asked as he sat down across from me. "It makes you look like a fuckin' wannabe soldier."

"Because the effort is what's important," I told him. "It sets me apart, says something about me."

"Yeah," Landry laughed. "Says you're a goddamn idiot." He laughed at that, but his mirth was short lived. We ate in silence after that.

Just as I was finishing my second slice of freshly thawed apple pie, the doors to the mess hall opened and Morris walked in with Simone at her side. Habits I thought I had dropped years ago brought me to my feet, though I did manage to keep from calling the room to attention.

"At ease, sergeant," she said crisply. "We leave at dawn, ladies and gentlemen. I can't promise a safe trip, but I can assure you it won't be boring. So, I'm unlocking the liquor cabinet a little. There is beer for everyone…over twenty one, that is," she hastily corrected herself with a look at Amy. "Limit two to a person." There was a collective moan at that, but no one stayed in their seat once the tub was rolled in. I grabbed my two bottles and went back to sit next to Amy. A chorus of pops and hisses filled the room as bottle tops were twisted off. Without a word, I set the first bottle in front of Amy and twisted the top off the second one.

"What's this?" she asked.

"Yours, if you want it," I told her. "I figure you had to deal with all the bullshit of growing up too early, you might as well get to enjoy some of the other parts." She grinned and twisted the top off, then held it up toward me. We let the bottles clink together before we both went to take a drink.

I saw Amy's hand move before I registered that Landry was reaching for her beer. Her palm smacked lightly against the back of his wrist, and she lowered the bottle to give him a glare as he drew back his arm. He sat there for a second, his face screwed into a foul look, then he came to his feet. We came up to meet him, and in spite of having a good six inches of height on me, and even more on Amy, he took a half step back. The room went silent as we faced each other across the table, everyone seeming to wait for one of us to make a move.

"The kid's not old enough," Landry said, his voice petulant. "You heard the boss."

"My kid," I said slowly, "my call. You got a problem with that, go tell your mommy." He went red faced as a few snickers reached our ears.

"She's not your kid," he spat. "You're just-"

"Landry!" McGregor cut him off. He turned to face the older agent with a glare, but McGregor was immune to it. "That's enough, son." With a final hard look my way, Landry grabbed his other beer and headed to the other end of the table.

"I'm really starting to not like that guy," I said as we took our seats.

"I could've taken him," Amy said with mock confidence.

"That's a question I could living without knowing the answer to," I said as McGregor walked our way. He sat down across from us and took a swig of his beer.

"Cut Landry a little slack," he said. "Boy's lost a lot of friends the past few weeks. He was just getting serious about a gal who worked on the First Lady's staff, too. We listened to Air Force One go down the second day. He took that pretty hard."

"We've all lost people," I said. "But I'll cut him some slack the minute he ditches that attitude."

"He's grieving. Dr. Parsons said he's probably going to be angry for a little while, then he'll get over it." Amy got up and stalked off without a word, her face set. "What's wrong with her?" McGregor asked.

"She watched her father jump out of a helicopter to save her life a couple of weeks ago," I said calmly. "Asking her to cut Landry some slack because he's a little fucked up over his girlfriend doesn't hold water with her, I'm guessing."

"I can see that," McGregor said with a slow nod. "It's been hard on everyone."

"Yeah," I said, looking around for a moment before I checked the clock on the wall. "I need to get to a radio," I muttered to myself.

"You can't just go making calls on our comm gear," he said.

"I brought one of my own," I said with a tight grin. "I made a promise to some folks back in Nebraska." McGregor stood when I did and followed me out into the hallway. Amy was leaning against the wall, holding the empty beer bottle in her left hand while she rubbed at her eyes with her right. I pretended not to notice the red splotches on her cheeks and her puffy eyelids.

"What now?" she asked.

"We're going topside to call St Mark's." She smiled at that and fell in beside me, giving McGregor a curious glance.

"I'm tagging along to make sure you don't compromise opsec," he grumbled as he pushed the door to the ops center open. "And to make sure you don't bust the damn radio. Your gear and your bikes are already packed. I'm too tired to deal with breaking it out and getting it stowed again." I grabbed the Shadowfire's case and headed for the door on the far side of the room. All of the comm gear had been disconnected from the antenna array, so we were going to have to set it up on our own. Lugging the case up the stairs wasn't quite as hard as it might have been one upon a time, but I was still a little winded by the time I got to the doorway behind the sculptures. The heavy steel portal let in a rush of cool air that made my nose tickle as I got to smell the outdoors for the first time in a couple of days. We emerged from the tunnel into twilight, and followed the beam of our flashlights to a metal ladder that led onto the top of the ridge.

From the top of Mt Rushmore, we could see for miles. Most of the world was covered in shadow, but the horizon was a stark line of black against the fading violet sky. For a moment, we gawked at the view, unable to ignore the majesty of the Black Hills. Off to the east, I could see the evening star shining bright in the sky. I knew it was really a planet, but I wasn't sure which one. A few weeks ago, all I would have had to do was look it up on the internet. Now, all I could do was wonder and feel a little overwhelmed by all the things I suddenly realized I didn't know.

Amy's hug pulled me out of my ruminations, and I looked down at her. She grinned when she saw my face and stepped back. "For a minute there," she said softly, "everything felt…okay. Like I was on the coolest road trip ever." I nodded and chuckled in spite of myself.

"Next time, we have to bring your mom," I said as I set the radio down.

"We'll have to bring her a t-shirt or something." She clambered up onto a crag of rock and looked west, leaving McGregor to hold the flashlight while I set up the portable dish.

"You make a pretty decent father," he said as I fiddled with the dish.

"Now, yeah," I said. "Point the light a little more to the left…thanks. Before Zompoc Monday? Not so much. Most parents taught their kids things like…God, I don't even *know* what they taught them. But now? I'm teaching her how to use a sword, how to field strip and clean a pistol…how to kill zombies. It's a really screwed up world where *I'm* a good role model." I worked in silence after that as I aligned the dish toward the satellite I needed.

Twenty minutes later, I was on the air.

"Magic Man, this is Lucky," McKay's voice answered on my third call. "How was your trip?"

"Not so bad," I said. "No one was on the roads. Is Coach back?"

"Yeah," her voice came back, suddenly less cheerful. "But the news isn't all good. Hang on, I'll get him."

"Dave," George's voice came a few moments later. "How ya doin' son?"

"Pretty fair," I said. "Allie says you've got unpleasant news." Amy's boots sounded on the rocks as she came closer.

"Some good, mostly bad," he said. "We found the farm, but by the time we got there...hell, son, there's no good way to say it. The parents were dead, and so were two of the kids."

"Which two?" I asked, my voice suddenly tight. Behind me, Amy let out a soft sob.

"Tad and Molly, the oldest boy and the youngest girl. We're still not sure what happened. The two who were still there are pretty traumatized. I'll spare you the details, but..."

"Don't," I said. "Tell me everything."

"Not much to tell. When we got there, there were four graves dug beside the house. The boy...he hides most of the time. The older girl hasn't said much. Mostly she just curls up in a ball and mutters. From what the Doc got out of her, the old man went after the youngest girl, and the older boy shot him. Then the mother stabbed the boy, and the oldest girl got momma from behind. Sounds like the two kids...they took a long time dyin', Dave. What we found in that house...I'm gonna be seein' it every time I close my eyes."

"I'm sorry, George," I said. I let up on the transmit key and bowed my head.

"Don't you apologize, son," he said. "There wasn't anything else you could have done. I asked myself a hundred times on the trip back if there was anything I would have done differently in your shoes."

"Well, for what it's worth...Lena did better than most people would have. I wish I'd been able to go back."

"I'll tell her you said that. But don't you worry. We'll take good care of them. You just get to where you need to go." As his words faded, I could see the gleam of tears on one cheek as Amy turned and walked a few steps away.

"Will do, Coach. Magic Man, out." I shut the radio down and gestured to McGregor to stay next to it as I walked toward Amy. Her head turned slightly as I got closer.

"Do you remember when I asked you how you dealt with having to kill people?" she asked as she reached over and took my hand. "Well, I know what I'm willing to kill for."

"Is it something you're willing to die for, too?" I asked.

"If I have to," she said. "A lot of the stupid shit you do makes a lot more sense now." She leaned her head on my shoulder.

"I'm glad it makes sense to somebody," I said.

Morning came way too soon, which I'd noticed it had a bad habit of doing. Since we were going to be outside the bubble today and heading deeper into zombie country, I went with my black cargo pants and t-shirt instead of the Park Ranger dress uniform. We were halfway into our armor when we noticed everyone watching us.

"You know we're going to be inside armored cars, right?" Caldwell said as she put her hair up into a tight bun at the back of her head.

"We have to get out some time," I said. "Like at the end of the day, or if we stop to fuel up."

"I'm sure as hell not sleeping in one of those things," Amy said. She held her right arm out to me and I laced her vambrace up.

"They're just trying to compensate for something," Landry said. That got a few laughs. The ribbing lasted until we put our body armor on and picked up the swords.

"Do you bring a knife to a gun fight?" Armstrong asked with a grin.

"Never jams, never misfires, never runs out of ammo," I said.

"Never been used, either," Landry said. Amy turned and moved toward him. McGregor moved to stop her but I put a hand on his arm and shook my head. This needed to be dealt with, but not by me, no matter how much I wanted to handle it myself.

"Have you ever killed a zombie with a knife?" she asked softly.

"I never let any get that close," Landry sneered.

"Ever fought any with your bare hands?"

"No," he said incredulously.

"We have," she said and turned her back on him. A chorus of jeers rose around him, and he stalked off after a few seconds. McGregor looked at Amy, then at me with a newfound respect in his eyes.

"How many has she killed with a sword?" he asked.

"At least ten," I said. "She also saved my ass when she shanked a ghoul, then she spiked it to finish it off."

Caldwell fell in next to Amy as we filed out of the barracks room, and McGregor stayed next to me. "You'll be in Stagecoach Two to start with," he said as we walked into the garage area. "Come end of day, I want you scouting ahead on your bike for a good place to set up for the night. If we have to stop, you do the dismount."

"So, that's a no to the comic relief, huh?" I said.

"You've been out in zombie country for the past three weeks, so you're either lucky as hell, or you know your shit. I don't care which, as long as you get the job done." He pointed toward the lead vehicle before peeling off toward the second car. I headed for it, and felt my gut clench as I saw Landry waiting beside it with his P90 cradled in his hands. He pointed at me, then crooked his finger at me. I held up one finger then headed over to pick up a P90 of my own from the rack. He stood glowering at me as I came up to him.

"That was pretty chickenshit back there," he muttered as I stopped in front of him. "Letting a little girl do your talking for you."

"Your first mistake," I said softly, "is not taking her seriously. Your second is assuming she was defending me." He frowned at me as I climbed into the Guardian. Armstrong was already in the front seat by the driver, and he pointed me to the seat behind him. Once I stowed my gun, I planted my butt in the seat and pulled my helmet off.

"You're gonna get awful hot in all that," one of the other agents said.

"I'd rather sweat than bleed," I answered while I pulled my *shemagh* from inside my vest and did a basic bandana tie around my head. With the Secret Service radio earplug in, I could hear the other drivers checking in as everyone loaded up. Once the last vehicle was ready, I heard McGregor's voice come over the radio.

"This is Stagecoach One taking primary call sign, we are ready to depart," he said.

"This is Stagecoach Two, taking Tracer," Armstrong said over his radio.

"Stagecoach Three, taking Halfback," Caldwell said. In front of us, Landry pressed a button on a standing console, and the metal door slid to one side to reveal a long tunnel that lit up as we moved forward.

"I thought we were Stagecoach Two," I said to Armstrong as Landry crouched in the vehicle hatch behind me.

"Those are our roles," Armstrong said, looking over the seat as we drove. "Tracer is the lead vehicle, Stagecoach is the President's vehicle and Halfback is the follow vehicle." We slowed as we approached a concrete wall, and Landry jumped clear of the hatch. My skin started to crawl a little, so I grabbed my helmet and went to the gun rack to retrieve my P90 about the time Armstrong turned to tell me to cover him.

"Open the back hatch," I said while I paused at the side hatch. "We'll come back in that way." The other agents barely hesitated as I jumped clear of the Guardian, and I heard the hatch closing up behind me. Landry looked back over his shoulder at me, but aside from a frown and a quick gesture for me to move to the left, he seemed to be the consummate professional.

"Clear the left side," he said, then he hit the control panel. This door dropped into the floor, and I brought my gun up to my shoulder as the edge came down to eye level. I scanned both sides as the motors whined, and saw someone standing off to the right of the door in a pair of shredded pajama bottoms. Without thinking, I stepped forward, brought the P90 up and put a round center mass. The strange tension at the back of my neck eased a little but didn't dissipate.

"What the fuck?" Landry hissed.

"Contact right, ghoul," I said. "Don't worry little brother...there are more." As the door came level with the ground, I stepped forward and swung my weapon to the left. When nothing leaped out in front of me, I keyed the mic on my new radio. "We have dead in the garage," I said softly.

"Landry, can you confirm?" Armstrong asked.

"Negative," Landry said. "He dropped one, but I don't see any- Wait a second...I think we have a survivor." I froze as I heard a faint voice in the distance. When I didn't hear it again, I took a slow step forward, still scanning left and right. "Did you hear that, Stewart?" he asked as he matched my movement.

"I heard something," I said. "Don't know what it was. But I know there's at least one more infected in here." We moved forward another few steps, and I could see that we were in the parking garage near the front gate of the park. Nothing moved but my instincts were practically screaming at me. Then, I heard it.

"Hello?" a woman's voice said. "Is anyone there?"

"We hear you," Landry called out, but my hackles went up.

"Hello?" she said again. A figure stepped into the light from behind a column only a few feet from us, and Landry lowered his weapon. She was lit from behind, so all I could see was a dark silhouette, but something still didn't feel right. The shape was right for a woman, and her arms and legs looked whole. Nothing looked out of place, but she also didn't look right, somehow.

"Tracer, we've made contact with another survivor," he said into his wrist mic as he took a step forward. "Ma'am, over here." She turned and let out a giggle that sent a shiver down my spine.

"Hello?" she said again, and it finally clicked in my head. She had said the same word three times in a row, and all three times, it had sounded *exactly* the same. I brought my gun up as Landry stepped forward, almost into my line of fire.

"Landry, move!" I said as she tensed. He turned his head my way, and the woman crouched a little. With a desperate titter, she launched herself at Landry. I let go of the gun and threw myself forward to hit her in midair, but her momentum knocked me back into Landry, and we all went tumbling. My gun hit the ground about the same time we did, and I pushed her away from me with my right arm as I groped at my belt for my knife. My fingers closed around the Tainto's grip as her giggle turned into a feral scream, and she grabbed my forearm. Her mouth opened to emit a putrid stench and she bent her head toward my wrist.

Behind me, Landry was yelling something, but I could barely hear him over the ghoul's screeching.

Her teeth inched closer to the soft point in my armor, the place where my wrist was only protected by the leather of my glove, and I got my knife up in front of me. My left hand drove forward, and the point of the knife slid into her left eye. Vitreous fluid mixed with black blood gushed across my glove and the knife hilt, and the ghoul fell silent with a gasp. When I pushed her away, she stayed there this time.

"What. The. Actual. FUCK!" Landry yelled. We heard feet pounding the concrete behind us, and got to our feet to find ourselves facing the barrels of four more guns.

"Are you guys okay?" Armstrong asked. "Did she bite you?"

"I'm good," Landry said quickly. He raised his hands to show no blood or bite marks on his arms. Everyone's aim shifted to me.

"Stewart, what about you?" Armstrong asked. I looked at him with ghoul eye goo dripping from my arm and the knife and grimaced.

"She slimed me," I said. For a few seconds, silence reigned, then Armstrong laughed, just a chuckle at first that grew into a full out belly laugh.

"You," he said between guffaws, "are one fucking hard core nerd. Caldwell, bring the decon kit from the truck, please," he finished into his wrist mic.

Forty minutes later, after spending half that time under the watchful eyes of Armstrong and half of the Secret Service team getting my hands and armor scrubbed down, we were back in the vehicle and emerging into the sun. Across from me, Landry was ashen faced and quiet.

"How'd you know she was…one of them?" he asked after a few minutes of watching the road twist and turn.

"Mostly it was the way she talked," I said. "She kept saying the same thing, and at the last, I realized she was saying it exactly the same way every time. Like a recording."

"You saved my ass," he said. "Thanks."

"No worries," I told him.

For the next half hour, we rode in silence. To get out of the Black Hills National Forest, we had to follow a small road that ran behind the monument through some of the most majestic country in America. Forested mountainsides loomed over us on either side of the road, reminding me of how small we were by comparison. Eventually, we hit Highway 16 and turned south. With every inch of road we covered, I wished I could see Amy's face, and wondered if she could even see any of this. Armstrong pointed to our left as we approached a stop light long the road.

"Over there, that's the Crazy Horse Memorial," he said. He handed me a pair of binoculars. "Pop that back hatch and keep your eyes peeled on our nine o'clock. If there are any infected in the area, this is where they'd likely be." The rear roof hatch slid open smoothly and let in a rush of cool air. When I popped up to look around, my eyes took a moment to adjust to the unfiltered sunlight. I took a moment to scan the area around us before I took a few seconds to focus on the Crazy Horse monument itself. Then my eyes were back on the road again.

"Nothing on our flanks," I reported.

"Get back inside and button up," Armstrong said. "We have contact forward." I dropped down and slid the hatch shut, then dogged it and clambered to the seat behind Armstrong. Up ahead I could see four pickup trucks waiting, two on either side of the road. Something about the arrangement seemed a little too obvious.

"Scan the citizen's band frequencies," I said. Armstrong fumbled at the radio, so I leaned forward and punched in the command. Seconds later, I heard a burst of static, followed by a voice speaking softly.

"They've seen us...they're slowing down. They're almost even with you....get ready."

"Stop!" Armstrong ordered. "Cover flanks!" Behind me, I heard the turret's servos whine as it traversed. "Stagecoach, cover flanks. We are boxed!" he called over the radio.

"Rafe, they stopped," the CB blared. "Get behind 'em and go for the truck. Kill the driver or shoot the tires and engine."

"Fire both guns," Armstrong said. "Light the side of the road up." Overhead, the M2 and the grenade launcher pounded away, and from the small window in the hatch, I could see a string of explosions along the side of the road going toward our rear. An orange blossom of flame went up as a round found something flammable and set it off. Orders flew and we surged forward. Up ahead, I could see the trucks back up and try to retreat, but Armstrong wasn't having any of it. Our gunner blew the lead truck on the right into oblivion with a trio of forty millimeter rounds, then punched a series of holes in the one behind it with the machinegun.

"Stagecoach Three, you're in the middle," McGregor said over the radio. "Stagecoach Two, you still have Tracer." The diesel rumbled as we got up to speed and I watched the four pyres of the would-be bandits as we passed them. I shook my head, amazed at how humans were still preying on each other in spite of the greater threat of the undead.

We followed a county road around Custer, then got back on 16 and followed it west, crossing into Wyoming by nine A.M. It took us out of our way by about fifty miles, but once we rounded a curve in Newcastle and turned south onto US 85, the next town was eighty miles due south of us, with nothing but straight, flat and empty road between us and it. Around noon, we hit the edge of Niobara county and saw a hand painted sign under the county limit sign. "All survivors must report to the Niobara Safe Zone upon entering county. Proceed to Niobara Women's Correctional Center IMMEDIATELY!" it read. Below it, in smaller letters, was the line "By order of President Shaw." We pulled to a stop a few feet from the sign and Armstrong leaned forward.

"Stagecoach, looks like we have a bunch of folks backing the wrong horse," he said into his mic.

"I see that," McGregor's voice came back over the main radio. "Stewart, I want you to scout the way ahead. The only thing that matters is getting our package to her destination, you clear on that?"

"I got it," I said.

"Better you than me," Landry said as I grabbed my M4. Once I was outside, it took a few minutes to get my bike off the back of the truck. Amy joined me as I was putting the M4 in its scabbard.

"I should be going with you," she said.

"You're the only other person who can feel when infected are nearby," I said. "And, your mother would kill me if you didn't make it."

"You can't keep using that excuse forever, you know."

"It's still working. But, the other reason is more important. Plus, none of these folks is going to let a teenager go into a potential fight." I tucked the USGS map McGregor had given me into the clear section on top of the tank bag and gave him a brief wave before I turned back to Amy. "Don't worry, I'll be back pretty quick."

"You better be," she said. Before she could say anything else, I hit the gas and headed out. The land around me was still green in places, and the rolling hills broke up the horizon a little. On the plus side, if there was anyone coming my way, I was going to see them a mile off. Of course, the other side of that was also true: I was going to be highly visible to anyone out here. For about twenty minutes, it was pure countryside, with surprisingly few cars on the road. Like a lot of the areas I'd been traveling through lately, though, Wyoming was sparsely populated. Even this near a town, traffic would have been thin at any point, to say nothing of an all-out evacuation. As I got further from the caravan, the constant nag in the back of my head eased, which told me they'd decided to drag the Alpha Zombie with us, but it also meant there weren't any nearby, which was a big relief.

Niobara City came into view when I was about a mile or two out, settled in a low spot surrounded by hills. The artificially green grounds of a cemetery were just starting to brown up as I passed the city limits sign that proclaimed Niobara City's population at fifteen hundred forty seven. A propane seller and a garage marked the first actual buildings in town, then I was into town proper. An overpass loomed ahead of me, and I slowed to a stop as I near the summit. On the other side was a road block of sorts, two cars, two trucks, a handful of motorcycles and a set of sawhorses set across the roadway. Ten men stood behind the wooden barriers, all of them sporting civilian hunting rifles.

"Stagecoach, this is Road Runner," I said into my radio mic as I pulled the binoculars out of the tank bag and focused on the men below me. "I've been spotted. The locals have a checkpoint on the main road into town. Looks like my job description just changed." Below me, the men were pointing at me and gesturing for me to come down. I looked left and right to see what was visible from my vantage point, then looked forward again.

"Copy on the road block, Road Runner," McGregor said. "What do you mean about the job description?"

"My new job is going to be a distraction. I'll meet up with you about five miles south of town in about an hour."

"Negative, Road Runner. Get out of there and we'll find an alternate route."

"They've seen me," I said as I lowered the binoculars and waved at the men. A single gunshot rang out and asphalt peppered my leg as the round hit a few feet away from me. "If I rabbit now, they're going to chase me." I cringed away from where the shot hit, and one of the men snatched the rifle from the man who had fired, then stepped out from behind the barricade and started walking toward me. I set the mic on open transmit and rode down toward the man, meeting him a few yards away from the rest.

"The last son of a bitch that shot at me is rotting on the side of the road about a hundred miles from here!" I said as I pulled my helmet off.

"I'm sorry about that," the lead man said as he closed the distance to me. He was tall and lean, with weathered features that looked like they'd seen years of wind and sun. He wore a brown jacket and jeans, with a cowboy hat that looked like it had seen almost as much time outside as its owner had. He had a hunting rifle slung on his left shoulder and a Sam Browne belt that sported a pistol and several magazine pouches. "Name's Miles Davis," he said as he reached out with one gloved hand. His grip was firm, but I got the feeling it wasn't as hard as he could make it.

"Nick Vincent," I said, using a pen name I'd considered.

"Well, Mr. Vincent, you mind if I ask why you aren't already in one of the Safe Zones?" he drawled.

"Because, as far as I know, there aren't any in North Dakota," I said with a smile. "I could ask the same of you, seeing as how the nearest one I can think of is in Colorado or Missouri."

"Not any more. The nearest Safe Zone is right here," he said proudly.

"I saw your sign, but a board and some paint don't make you a Safe Zone." I watched his face as I said that, but he just smiled.

"President declared us 'bout a week ago. He's been all over the radio with the updated list. We also have our credentials, signed by the man himself. I can promise you, son, you're about as safe as you can get now." He gestured toward the row of men, one of whom was holding up a set of papers.

"You mind if I have a look at those?" I said as I dismounted the bike and started pushing it. He started back toward the others with me, and I took the set of papers from the man holding them up. Sure enough, it looked official, complete with seals embossed on the paper. Another man gestured to Miles, and he left me with the man who'd been carrying the official documentation.

"How'd they get this to you?" I asked.

"Air drop," the man said. This guy was wearing almost the same outfit, with the same kind of belt and holster. Only his jacket was different, a wool-lined tan leather. "If we need medicine or ammo or anything like that, they send a drone to drop it off. Hell, about the only thing that didn't come by drone is Agent Coffey over there." He leaned in and said softly, "And as far as I'm concerned, they can have his ass back. Worthless sonofabitch don't do nothing but complain and eat." I laughed at that and looked toward the man he had gestured at. Most of the men wore variations of the same rancher's outfit, with baseball caps or cowboy hats. Coffey wore a long black duster and a wool watch cap. A gust of wind blew the bottom of his duster to the side and I could see a tactical holster on his right leg. He was showing Miles something and pointing at me, but Miles was shaking his head. He turned to look over his shoulder at me, then turned back to Coffey with a disbelieving look on his face.

"He looks pissed about somethin'," I said.

"He's always lookin' for some wanted person or another," the man beside me said. "Hell, he went through everyone in town trying to find people in that stupid Most Wanted deck of his."

"I don't see any infected," I said as the exchange between Coffey and Davis started to get more heated.

"There weren't that many to start off," he said. "We set up the speakers over at the fair grounds and started playing music as loud as we could, shooting off fireworks at night to get them all over that way. After that, it was a turkey shoot, know what I mean?" I was about to make a comment when Coffey unslung his rifle. From forty or fifty yards away, I could see that it was some variant of an M4, all tacti-cooled out with more junk than he'd ever need.

"You!" he shouted. "Evan Reynolds! Hands in the air where I can see them!" I blinked as I tried to process what he was saying. Who in the hell was Evan Reynolds?

"I told you," I called back to him as I held my hands out to the side, "my name's Nick Vincent. Let me get my ID out of the tank bag here." I reached out with my left hand and let go of the official papers. For a split second, everyone's eyes followed the white fluttering pages as the wind caught them. My right hand hit the electric start and the bike roared to life as I straddled it, and I was mobile. I heard gunshots behind me as I leaned over the handlebars and yelled into the mic at my shoulder, "Stagecoach, go!"

When I looked behind me a few seconds later, I could see a couple of men on motorcycles already pulling out behind me. Coffey was leading the way on a black street bike. He was pulling ahead of the others and gaining on me pretty fast. I waited until he was only a few yards away from me before I turned hard to my right. Tires squealed in my six as Coffey braked, and I could see him straightening his bike and trying to gun the engine to catch up to me. My next turn was a left, and the another, which left me racing back the way I'd come. After the first block, I saw what I needed and turned left again at the next, coming out behind the rest of the local militia as they passed. Coffey followed, gaining again as we stayed on the straight-away, leaving the rest of the men with him far behind. After a few blocks, the road came to a T, and I could see the overpass I'd started the chase from. I took the left turn and followed the road as it curved around and passed over the railroad tracks. After the first building I passed on my right, I leaned hard into a right turn and went off-road, heading for a low hill I'd seen from the overpass. Coffey swung in behind me and gunned his bike as we raced toward the hill. He pulled up on my right, and I twisted the throttle a little more. His bike easily paced mine, and he turned his head toward me to give me a triumphant smile. I looked toward the hill and goosed the bike again. His head turned and he leaned forward over his handle bars as he poured on even more speed.

He hit the hill a second before I did, and we went airborne. A split second too late, he saw what I'd maneuvered him into, and I heard him scream. If he'd been a local, I would have felt bad.

On the other side of the hill were several low mounds of gravel and dirt in a straight line. My jump took me a few feet to one side of them, but he had jumped right at them, and there was no way he was going to land without crashing. His back tire hit the top of one and his bike flipped before it slammed into the one on the other side with a sickening crunch. I skidded to a stop and shut the bike off, then ran to the wreckage.

Coffey's head was twisted at an unhealthy angle, and his eyes were glassy and blank. I heard his radio squawking on his bike, and the sound of vehicles came from the west of us as I squatted down next to his body. Most of his gear was standard stuff for the guys I'd seen posing as Homeland Security: black tactical gear, most of it comparable to military issue. He had a Glock 31 and three spare mags in the tactical holster and a map case slung across his body. Most of it was of no interest to me, though his radio was an intel windfall and I unsnapped the map case. I grabbed his personal radio and checked his pockets, turning up an official looking government ID for Travis Coffey, and the deck of cards the local man had been talking about. The card that was facing up was for Evan Reynolds, a sour faced man who bore only passing resemblance to me. The card ID him as a follower of the Sovereign Citizen movement, though I doubted he was associated with them.

"Really?" I asked as I held the card up. "You mistook me for this guy? I look twice as good as he does." My next goal was what was left of his bike. The radio had survived relatively intact, and I paused for a moment. It was a model I'd never seen before, slimmer than most of the military issue comm systems I'd used. I grabbed it and pulled the mount it had been in as well, trusting that I'd be able to remember how it was wired.

"Road Runner, this is Stagecoach, we're clear of town. Heading to rendezvous point." McGregor's voice in my ear was a stark reminder that there was still more to do.

"Roadrunner copies, Stagecoach," I said softly.

"Agent Coffey, this is Davis, do you read me?" I heard Miles' voice come over both of the confiscated radios. As quickly as I could, I grabbed the assault rifle magazines from Coffey's vest and went to my bike, then drew the Five-seveN. When Miles repeated his call, I put a round through the wrecked bike's tank, holstered the pistol and pulled my survival tin from my vest. One of the wind-proof matches caught as I dragged it along the strip of sandpaper glued to the top, and I flicked it toward the growing puddle of gas before I started the bike and headed toward the overpass. The gas caught and the tank blew as I raced under the bridge. The radio went wild for a few minutes after that as they closed in on the rising column of smoke. Finally, Miles' voice came over the air.

"Homeland, this is Niobara," he said calmly. "Agent Coffey is dead. We have a rogue survivor heading east, Coffey thinks he was the two of spades. I'm requesting a drone overflight."

"Negative on drone overflight, Niobara," another voice came back a few moments later. "Two of spades is confirmed to be out of your area, negative on ID. Return to base, conserve your resources. Outside patrols are suspended for the next forty-eight hours to protect your teams. Do not venture outside your perimeter."

"Understood, Homeland. Heading back now." When the bigger radio squawked but the smaller one didn't, I braked to a stop and pulled it out of its case.

"Hightower, this is Homeland," I heard. "Task Overflight one-two Alpha to Niobara Safe Zone to ping an agent's sat-comm."

"Homeland, acknowledge, Overflight one-two Alpha retasking. ETA to target zone, ten minutes."

"Stagecoach, find cover," I hissed into the radio. "Drone incoming in ten. Find cover immediately and go radio silent." Without waiting for an acknowledgment, I turned my radio off and frantically checked the agent's radio. Its interface was very similar to a smart phone, and a minute or two later, I was scrolling through subscreens to find what they might be pinging. I killed the GPS feed but I suspected there was more. On the security screen, I found what I was looking for: an internal security monitor. The screen instructed the user to set it on the base unit, and I grabbed that from the tank bag.

"Not found," the screen reported when I plugged it in a few seconds later. I briefly wondered if taking it off the bike had shut down the part they were going to ping, if it was somehow separate from the radio mount, or if the phone would be able to respond to the security ping on its own. As the clock showed the drone getting closer and closer, I made a decision and opened the back of the phone and pulled the battery. Finally, I dumped the other radio and its components back into the map case, then hauled ass back to the overpass.

Chapter 9
Unknown Territory
~ Change is not a destination, just as hope is not a strategy ~
Rudy Guliani

I waited half an hour before I put the battery back in on the bigger radio. While I sat under the bridge, I went through the map case and the deck of most wanted cards. My face was on the jack of spades, and Amy was the three of hearts. Nate was the king of spades, and Col. Shafer made the ace of spades. Both Amy's card and mine had red X's drawn across them. There was also a small user's manual for the PC9 IntelSat interface I'd taken from Coffey's body. He'd scrawled his login and password inside the manual, and looking at the random series of numbers and letters, I couldn't blame him. Evidently, the system scanned for words or common number combinations and wouldn't let you use them in your password or log-in ID. Skimming through it, I developed a new level of respect for whoever had made this thing. Half cell phone, half computer and a hundred percent leading edge, the damn thing was smarter than I was. The ironic thing was that it was so smart that it was easy to use. Once I plugged the battery back in, I walked through the menu to put it in passive only mode, and started scanning the different data streams.

In passive mode, it accessed and decoded satellite feeds without showing up in their systems. After a few minutes of searching, I found the stream for drone one-two Alpha. It showed Niobara from above, and the thinning column of smoke from Coffey's wrecked bike. The view zoomed out and I could see that the drone was quite a ways from town.

"Homeland, nothing on eastern quadrant either," someone was saying. "He's gone, whoever he is."

"Affirmative, Hightower," another, deeper voice replied. "ELINT isn't picking up any radio traffic, either. This guy bugged straight the hell out. Return to Niobara, brass wants you to put ordnance on the bike."

"What about the zone?" the first voice asked.

"Negative on the safe zone. Just the bike."

"Affirmative. Launching Griffin." Seconds later, an explosion rocked me as the Griffin missile hit its target and threw dirt and debris into the air. Rock and soil pelted the ground for several seconds, then the voice on the radio came back

"Confirmed hit, Hightower. It's toast. Return to sector patrol." Hightower confirmed the order and started away. Once the GPS locater put it far enough out for my comfort, I turned my radio back on

"Stagecoach, this is Roadrunner, you got your ears on?" I said.

"Roadrunner, this is Stagecoach, we read you," McGregor's voice came back.

"Got some new intel. Drone's gone. I'm heading south, see you there." I started the bike and pulled out from under the bridge. The graying sky looked more ominous and there was a damp feel to the wind in my face as I hit the roadway and sped along the main street. Stagecoach was waiting for me near the county fairgrounds on the south side of town, and I pulled up beside the lead vehicle. The vehicle commander's hatch opened on the roof and McGregor's head popped up as I put the kickstand down.

"Stow your bike and get in. The boss wants you on board," he said.

With the help of two other agents, I got the bike loaded back onto the truck, and crawled into Stagecoach One. "You rang, Madam Prez?" I said as I took the seat across from her.

"Tell me what happened," she said simply. As much as I wanted to start with a snappy one liner, I figured it was bad form to give the President any more attitude. For about half an hour, I was as boring as I'd ever been as I related the events back to her and showed her the PC9. That got taken from me the moment I pulled it out of the bag.

"I'll need to find someone who can do a more thorough analysis of this," she said as she went to hand it off.

"Like a Communications Signals Intelligence Specialist?" I asked while I pointed at myself. "That's pretty much my job description, ma'am. If you're going to draft me, you might as well let me do what I was trained for." She turned a narrow eyed gaze on me for a few seconds before she gave a speculative "Hmmm," and handed the device back to me.

"Are you always this insubordinate with your superiors?" she asked coolly.

"Only when they need to hear it, ma'am," I said. She smiled and leaned back.

"So, what is your take on this group at the prison?" she asked.

"Basically, they're a bunch of regular folks just trying to be good citizens, ma'am," I said after a moment. "They want to do the right thing, and I figure Shaw's telling them what they need to hear. The drone operator asked about hitting the safe zone, so I figure that's happened more than once when someone got out of line or something."

"Why haven't we heard about it?" Morris asked.

"Probably because there's no one left alive to say anything," I offered as I pulled out the Most Wanted deck. "They also have their own little hit list." She took it and flipped through it.

"I see you and Amy made the list," she said while she was looking through the deck. "I'm a little disappointed that I didn't, but I can only guess that's because they think I'm dead."

"They'll come out with a new one the moment they find out different," I said. "Poor Col. Shafer is likely to get demoted to King of Spades to make room for you."

"I'd pass on the honor if I could," Morris said. She turned to the bespectacled doctor in the seat beside her. "Anita, do you have any questions to ask Sergeant Stewart?"

"Well, there is the obvious," Parsons said as she pushed the narrow lensed glasses up on her forehead. "Did you sense any infected while you were in town?"

"Not that I noticed, but I was a little distracted," I said. "One of the local men said they had rounded them all up at the local fair grounds. I got the impression they had killed them all after that."

"Hmm...well, with the results I got from your tests, I wanted to see if there was a chemical component to your abilities."

"What results?" I asked.

"I exposed your blood to the Asura virus samples we got from Miss Bach," she said with more emotion than I'd seen from her since I'd met her. "The results were...dramatic, to say the least, but inconclusive on a fresh sample. That, of course, was also against a sample from an alpha level subject. I'd like to see what kind of reaction I get from a first or second stage subject, and see if my theory about the virus is correct."

"Do you know what caused it?" I asked.

"No," she laughed. "I don't have nearly enough data for that. But based on the results of the tests I ran, I think it would take a little longer for the Asura virus to turn you."

"How much longer?" Amy asked from her seat at the back.

"Maybe six hours," Dr. Parsons said with a shrug. "Though that is the most optimistic guess. Four hours would be more likely. All I had was equipment that was outdated in the Sixties. There were no living cells left in the samples I used, and I don't know what the effect against a stage one or two bite would be. But I do have to ask, have either of you been exposed to the virus in another way? Scratches, blood splatter from infected or even close physical contact?" We both nodded.

"This morning was a pretty good example," I said.

"That might explain it. You both have elevated white blood cell counts, indicative of an immune response. I don't know if it's your body's response to limited exposure to the Asura virus, or if it really is something in your genetic makeup that is causing the response. Either way, it's intriguing."

"You say intriguing, I say scary as shit," Amy said.

"I suppose so," Parsons said. "Once we stop, though, I'd like to get some more blood samples." I shrugged. If Morris gave the word, technically, I didn't have a choice. My oath of enlistment was less than forty-eight hours old, and it was already becoming a bigger pain in my ass than I liked.

We headed west from Niobara, taking side roads to Highway 25, until we were back on the vast empty plains, bare of all but the scarcest signs that mankind had even walked the world. For once, we rode safe and secure, and I wasn't driving. But relaxing was not the first thing on the agenda. It was time for me to do what I'd been trained for. The comm-sat's interface was pretty intuitive, and before long, I was able to tap into Homeland's signal again. For half an hour, I monitored radio traffic, but nothing seemed to have them too concerned. With nothing out of the ordinary to worry about, I sat back, pulled The Fuzzy Files from my right cargo pocket and took advantage of the first chance to read that I'd had for almost three weeks.

I barely noticed when we skirted a little town called Wheatland, and only emerged from Piper's world of Zarathustra when we pulled to a stop at the junction of state highway 287. The rear end of a blue sedan stuck up from the far side of the railroad tracks, leaving a trail of tire ruts and debris where it had left the road.

"Okay folks, let's stop here for a few, stretch the kinks out and grab a bite," McGregor said. He turned to me and gestured for me to lean closer. "Can you use that sat-comm to see where their drones are?" he asked quietly.

"Yeah, I can pull up their individual feeds and ping a GPS position from their telemetry," I said. "But they're always moving, so anything I get is going to be a rough guess."

"We just need to find out if they have anything moving our way."

"That, I can do," I said. It only took a few seconds to tap back into the network while the rest of the team secured the area to find what he needed. He frowned when he saw the expression on my face.

"Why do I get the feeling I'm not going to like what I'm about to hear?" he asked.

"Because you're right," I said as I brought up the feed. "There is a drone headed this general direction. If we try to head west and go through the National Forest, odds are good it'll pick us up. But…" I showed him the drone's camera feed. Clouds piled high on one another, and the view shifted as the camera focused on something else.

"They're heading west to avoid the weather," he said. As if to agree with him, a low rumble of thunder came from the south. "So we'll head south to take advantage of it. Grab something to eat and then get your gear under a tarp or in the truck." Everyone was lining up at the back of the truck, and I went to check it out. Caldwell and Armstrong were handing out box lunches. Amy was near the front of the line, and I saw that she grabbed two, then came back to me.

"There's ham and cheese or cheese and ham, take your pick," she said, thrusting one of the boxes at me.

"So much for the kosher menu," I said as I took the box. "Damn, this is cheese and ham…I wanted the ham and cheese." Amy took a big bite out of her sandwich then looked at me with her mouth full.

"T'ff rookk," she mumbled around her food.

"Big bully," I said.

"You know what I'd love more than anything right now?" she asked as the wind picked up and chilled our exposed skin. "A bowl of Mom's chili."

"I'd settle for just seeing her again," I said as I looked west. We ate quietly, then went to the vehicles and made sure our packs were under the tarp before we loaded back up. Half an hour after we had stopped, we were headed south on 287 toward Laramie. Ahead of us, the sky was getting darker, and we could see gray sheets of rain angling toward the ground. Lightning turned the clouds yellow inside, only occasionally escaping to lance toward the earth.

As the leading edge of the storm got closer, we started to see bright points of light that started to resolve themselves into headlights.

"What the hell?" Armstrong said as they got closer. I punched the radio to the citizens' band and started scanning. Seconds later, channel nineteen blared to life.

"..head south. Do *not* head south. This is Uncle Fester on highway two-eight-seven. If you're anywhere near Laramie, Wyoming, you gotta head north, east west, it don't matter. Just don't go south." I handed Armstrong the mic.

"Uncle Fester, what's going on?" he asked.

"There's a fuckin' wall of fuckin' zombies headed north. I was in Denver, and I never saw nothin' like it. They're all just walkin' north, even the fast ones. If you know what's good for you, get the fuck outta here. That ain't the half of it. They flushed a prison gang outta Greeley, bastards got a shitload of guns and rocket launchers from some damn place." By then, we could see the first of the vehicles coming toward us. Wet with rain, it passed us without slowing down. Further ahead, we saw a flare of yellow and then the black and orange blossom of a fireball floated up.

"Copy that. Listen, there's a safe zone north of here, little town called Niobara. Head to the Women's Correctional Center on the northwest side of town. You might be safe there."

"Ten-four," Uncle Fester said. If there was anything else on his mind, Armstrong didn't seem interested, since he switched to the Secret Service frequencies.

"Stagecoach One and Three, break west on...County Road 51. We have incoming tangoes, dead and alive. The live ones are well armed and willing to fire."

"Acknowledged, Stagecoach Two," McGregor's voice came back. "Break west on county five-one. All vehicles go weapons hot." Inside the vehicle, the agents reached for the black vests under their seats and grabbed P90s. Armstrong pointed to a sign on the right, and the driver pulled wide to the left and stopped with the truck across the road, nose pointed to the right. The turret servos whined as the gunner traversed left to cover the approach from the south. Through the small window in the door, I could see the supply truck and Stagecoach one turn down the road we had just passed.

"Stagecoach Two taking Halfback," Armstrong said as he leaned across the middle of the front seat. "We have-" he started, then the ping of bullets hitting the side of the vehicle cut him off. "Incoming," he finished .Overhead, the machinegun chattered, and we rolled forward again. The turret spun again and the grenade launcher thumped and more rounds smacked against the hull. I could see the other two vehicles pulling away from us, the dust kicked up from their passing also starting to obscure them.

"Saunders, whattya got?" Armstrong asked.

"I can't see anything behind us...wait...they're cutting across the field...two behind us...lighting 'em up!" Ma Deuce opened up again, and Saunders muttered "Gotcha!" under his breath. Then I heard bullets spang off the hull on my side, and I looked out to see an Escalade pull up beside us. The driver had his hand out the window, pulling the trigger on a small SMG. Behind him, another gang member in a blue bandana was leaning out the window with an AK in his hands, emptying the mag at the front window. A flame blossomed inside, then someone popped up on the far side with a Molotov in hand.

Not one to miss an opportunity when it presented itself, I opened the firing port and stuck my P90's stubby barrel through it, then pulled the trigger and angled it from left to right. Silver edged holes traced a ragged line just below the door handles, and the big SUV veered right as the driver slumped over the wheel. The top of the truck caught fire as it bounced, then the inside erupted into flames as well. Across the vehicle from me, another agent was firing at something, and I closed the firing port on my side so I could change mags. The Guardian was knocked forward, and the driver hit the gas.

"Contact rear," Saunders called down from the turret. "Trying to get a man on top!" Armstrong looked at me, and I headed for the rear door before he could utter a word, popping the magazine down on my SMG as I went. The rear door didn't have a firing port, so I had to unlock the upper hatch. It swung open on a beige Cadillac bearing down on our rear end. Another guy in a blue bandana was crouched in the open area where the windshield used to be, and the passenger pointed an assault rifle at us over the dash. The temptation was to spray a line of bullets across the front of the car, but McGregor's training stayed with me, and I put a short burst into the guy pointing the gun at me. Shots spanged off the hull all around me as he managed to squeeze the trigger, but I was already moving my aim to the driver. He got a longer burst, and the car started to slow and veer left. That left the guy on the hood, and he was showing a sudden dedication to the mission as he took two steps across the hood and tried to leap across the widening gap between our vehicles. As I brought the P90 to bear on him, we both realized that he wasn't going to make the jump. His mouth opened in a terrified scream as he fell a couple of feet short of the rear of my vehicle. He bounced once when he hit the dirt road, then disappeared under the front tires of his own car. I felt a moment of pity for him until a blue Lincoln swerved around it and tried to catch up to us. I put a long burst through the front grill, then a couple of short bursts into the front windshield, and it fell back. Nothing else came out of the dust cloud at us, so I pulled the hatch shut and dogged it again.

"That looks like the last of them," I called out as I made my way forward.

"Roger that," Saunders said. We sped up, and a few minutes later, we were catching up to the rest of our little convoy, and for the next hour, we drove with our eyes to the south and to the east. Our back trail to the east stayed clear, but the wall of clouds slowly rolled up on us.

When the rain hit, it came in almost vertical sheets that buffeted the vehicles on their shocks and left slowly spreading layers of frost on the windshields. When the supply truck nearly slid off the road, McGregor ordered us to a stop in the lee of a hill. We sat there for hours, pummeled by rain and ice as the sky slowly darkened. I checked my map, and fought to keep my cool as I traced out the distance to Nate's place. Less than twenty miles away, and all that stood between Maya and me was some water and cold air. That, and miles of ice slick roads.

I read more of The Fuzzy Files, and finally forced myself to close my eyes and catch a little sleep, since I couldn't do anything productive. When Armstrong finally said my name, I came up from dreams of desolate lands filled with the dead.

"Yeah," I said, bleary eyed and grateful to be awake. The Guardian's diesel engine rumbled to life and the interior lights went red.

"Storm's over. We're moving," he said. "There's a campground a couple of miles down the road. Mac says there might be a ranger station or something there we can rack out in." I grunted something that sounded like an agreement and rubbed the grit from my eyes as we started moving. Twenty minutes of slow, careful driving later, we were pulling into what I assumed was the campground. Two large buildings loomed on either side of the road, with a broad parking lot in front. One was a visitor's center, with a glassed in waiting area. Most of the glass was broken, and we could see bodies inside. The other building was a rectangle of cinderblock with only a couple of windows that I could see. A Park Services truck was parked beside it, the driver's door open.

"Stewart, you're with me," McGregor's voice came over the radio. Armstrong looked at me with an apologetic shrug.

"You're too good at what you do," he said.

"Work, work, work," I said as I grabbed my gun and popped the side hatch. A blast of cold air hit my lungs like an icicle, and

I pulled the tail of my shemagh around in front of my face and caught it between my teeth. McGregor was waiting for me with Landry and Amy behind him. Amy carried the Mossberg and tried not to look cold, but even in the dark, I could see her shoulders hunch as she fought to keep from shivering.

"She insisted," he said over the wind and engine noise when I looked from her to him and cocked my head. In the light of the Guardians' headlamps, I could see a slight mist still falling, but no other movement aside from us.

"Alright, but she's with me," I said. He shook his head and started to say something, and I cut him off. "Fine, *you* tell her to stick with Landry." He held up a hand and turned to Landry. They fell in step, and Amy settled into a spot just to my right. As we came closer to the building, I felt the familiar pressure building at the back of my head that meant more infected were close by. Amy's posture changed as we crept closer to the door, her shoulders dropping and her head inching forward. McGregor and Landry went to either side of the door, then Mac looked back at me.

"Infected," I said with a nod toward the door.

"See if there's another door," he said. We headed right and found another door on the other side of the building. I turned the tac light on my P90 on and shone it on the knob. A dark brown smear ran down the wall beside the door, and thin streaks of congealed blood were on the doorknob.

"We have a door. Keys in the lock," I radioed.

"Copy. Get ready to move in." I looked to Amy and nodded, and she slowly chambered a round while I switched the P90's fire selector to burst. From the other side of the building, we could hear a fist pounding on the door. Seconds later, a loud thump sounded against the same door, and we moved in. I kept my barrel pointed down to keep the light on the floor as we stepped into the doorway. A hallway led to our right, and a room opened up to our left. I got a vague sense of appliances along the wall that stretched out in front of us, and furniture off to my left as I focused on the sound coming from across the room. Rapid impacts against a door and a raspy growl told me where the infected was in general, and I brought the SMG up. The tactical light fell on a man in a park ranger uniform with the right half of

156

his face missing. He was turning to face us, his one eye wide and rolling.

Amy's shotgun boomed, and I felt the overpressure against my body as the shot caught the infected in the sternum and threw him against the door. I stepped forward and put the sight on his nose, then pulled the trigger. With his skull perforated and his chest shattered, I was pretty sure this one wasn't going to pull through, so I gestured with my right hand for Amy to cover the hallway to our right.

"Front room is clear," I said as I moved to the other side of the room and pointed down the other hallway. Nothing moved, so I nudged the dead ranger away from the door with my foot and reached across my body to open the door with my right hand. McGragor and Landry came in as I sidestepped to make room for them. At a gesture from Mac, Landry went to Amy's side. Mac moved in front of me and advanced down the hallway. We all came out in a bunkroom. Trash littered the floor, and one of the beds was stained with blood, but no other infected seemed to be waiting for us.

"This'll do," Mac said. "Saunders, Armstrong, clear the other building. Caldwell, get the package inside." He grabbed the bloody bedding and folded the mattress on itself, then picked the whole mess up. I led the way to the door I'd come in through, and he tossed the bundle off to one side. We hurried back and dragged the ranger's body out, taking it as far as we dared in the dark before we jogged back to the lodge. By the time we got back, Caldwell had Morris and the other civilians ushered into the bunk room. Another agent had brought a lantern in and I could see a fireplace against the far wall with wood and newspaper piled next to it on the stone hearth. The front room had an open kitchen that looked onto another fireplace that was surrounded by heavy chairs. Couches were set on opposite walls, and a boom box shared space with a TV on a low table against the same wall as the fireplace.

As more people started to file in, Mac took me to one side. "I know it's been a long day for you," he said. "But it isn't over yet. I want Amy to stay near the President tonight. You, me and a couple of other agents are going to stay in Stagecoach One and take shifts on watch."

"Can I at least eat before we bed down in the RV?" I asked. He gave a brief laugh at that. I tried to glare a hole in his back as he left me to tell Amy where she was going to be spending the night. *Twenty miles,* I told myself. *Twenty miles from Maya.* It might as well have been twenty light years.

An hour later, I found myself on watch in the Guardian's turret. A warm fire, a comfortable chair and a good meal were pleasant memories. I had tried to teach Amy how to play checkers, and ended up getting my ass kicked after the fourth game. Now she was asleep inside, and I was counting down the minutes to the end of my watch. Saunders and Landry were racked out on the floor below me, and McGregor was snoring in the front seat.

In this weather, it wasn't people we had to worry about, it was the dead. Mac's choice to have Amy near the president and me in the truck made a ruthless sort of sense. Both of us would know if infected were nearby long before anyone could see them, and we had a lot more experience in dealing with them than anyone else in the detail. It was the kind of brutal practicality I figured a Secret Service agent needed, and I had to respect it, even if I wasn't thrilled being on the pointy end of it.

For two hours, I sat there and dutifully listened to the cold wind hiss against the hull and the occasional splatter of rain. After a while, I let my mind wander, since the weird sixth sense that let me know when infected were around wasn't one I had to concentrate on. As my thoughts drifted, I felt myself settle into the semi-trance that my grandfather had showed me, aware but placid. After a few moments, I started to feel something similar to what I felt in Kansas City, some presence in the dark. This one wasn't searching though. It was a steady pulse, an insistent drumbeat calling out into the night. So far, though, I couldn't feel any other undead aside from the alpha in the truck nearby. Wyoming was almost as empty as Nebraska.

When my watch was done, I woke Saunders up and laid myself out on the sleeping bag he'd vacated, figuring I was never going to get to sleep. Not so close to Maya, so close to the end of the journey…

The dead were marching, heading toward some beacon that drew them, moving west. Occasionally one would slip on the roadway, then slowly get to its feet, some new damage showing. A broken arm, a leg that bent where it shouldn't, a foot that slewed sideways. The rain pelted them, blew them to the side, but always, they came, moving forward, toward the steady pulsing call, and insistent drumbeat calling out into the night...

I woke up to a wan light in the vehicle and a chill breeze on my face. The turret was empty, and I heard the wind moan outside. A metal clank brought me to full awareness, and I sat up. Across from me, Saunders was still asleep, and McGregor was stirring in the front seat.

"Where's Landry?" I asked. Saunders mumbled something before he opened his eyes and looked around. He yawned and propped himself up on one elbow before looking around.

"I woke him up for his watch. What time is it?" he said as he blinked sleep from his eyes.

"Sun's coming up," I said, getting to my feet and grabbing my pistols. Once the SOCOM and the Five-seveN were holstered, I grabbed the P90 and headed for the open rear hatch. With every step I took, a growing sense of dread was creeping up the back of my neck. The second my boots hit the ground, my head was moving, scanning right to left. Indistinct sounds were coming from behind the supply truck, and to my left I heard the door to the lodge open. Even before I looked that way, I knew Amy was coming out the door. Caldwell was beside her, with Morris in the rear.

"Get her back inside!" I snapped as I moved toward the truck. Caldwell turned and put an arm out, but her charge shook her head. Amy stepped away from them and started angling toward the back of the truck, her path taking her to the same place I was pointed. I could hear Saunders and McGregor moving behind me, but their concern was the President.

The tightness at the back of my neck slowly made its way down to the space between my shoulder blades as I came closer to the back of the truck. Something clanked in the back, metal on metal, and I gestured with my right hand for Amy to go a little further to cover me. I stepped around the back of the truck and pointed inside.

In the dim interior, something moved, and my tac light fell on Landry's face. His mouth was full as he reached for something, and his hand came back dripping with something brown and chunky. As I came around toward the middle, I could see open cans and wrappers on boxes and on the floor, and Landry's chin dripping with food.

"Hungry," he growled as the light fell back on his face. "I'm so hungry." His pupils were like pinpricks as he looked at me, his cheeks flushed and bright red. I'd seen something like this before.

"What the hell?" McGregor said as he came up beside me. A manic sounding giggle came from behind Landry, and I stepped to one side to see the alpha zombie's case sitting upright, the thick plexiglass scratched and the case dented.

"You're bad little monkeys," the thing that used to be Sarah Bach said. "Mister Landry, would you please kill the Nephilim and that feisty little bitch with him, and let me out of here?" For a moment, Landry hesitated, his eyes starting to focus on us.

"I swore an oath," he said slowly. "I shouldn't…Mac, she showed me things…showed me Crystal…there are…so many things…but…I have to…" He shook his head, then let out a scream and dove at McGregor. My right arm came up and shoved McGregor away and my left hand tightened on the P90's trigger a microsecond too late. Shoving McGregor to the side brought me just far enough into Landry's path that we went sprawling together, the P90 flying from my grip. For a moment, my right arm was numb from the impact, and I used the brief respite to grab the SOCOM from the holster and shove the slide up against Landry's back. Instead of trying to get free of him, I leaned in and pushed the gun forward, raking the slide across his shirt and chambering a round, then turned it and pulled the trigger as fast as I could.

Even that was a little too slow, and Landry tossed me to the side before I could empty more than five rounds into him. I rolled and staggered to my knees as Landry bounced to his feet. Again, there was a moment of hesitation, and Amy hit him with a round from the Mossberg. He staggered, and she pumped another round and shot him again. Then McGregor brought his pistol up and fired half a dozen times from the ground. Landry's body jerked with each impact, then he fell to his knees, blood soaking his shirt. He coughed once and pink froth flecked his lips before he pitched forward.

I got to my feet as the last echoes of gunfire faded. Then Landry moved, reaching one arm toward me and gasping my name. I was at his side in a split second.

"Coming…" he gasped. "They're coming…calling them…she's calling them." Then the light faded from his eyes and he fell back. I took a step back and pointed the SOCOM at his forehead, but my finger didn't tighten on the trigger. Something was different.

"He's dead," Amy said as she stepped up beside me. "I mean, I can't feel him. He just faded when he died." I nodded, understanding now that she'd said it. Feeling was starting to return to my right arm, and it was a change I wasn't all that grateful for.

"How?" McGregor asked. "They all go zombie after you kill them." I looked down at my right arm, then at Landry, and suddenly, I knew.

"Get her loaded on the Guardian," I said, pointing at the back of the supply truck. "Amy, get on your bike and get to Nate's place as fast as you can. You have to warn them. There's an army of infected headed this way. Mac, get everyone else loaded up and follow Amy as fast as you can. Get the President to Col. Shafer."

"What about you?" Amy asked. I looked at her and turned so she could see my right side, slowly holding up my bleeding right arm.

"I have to go the other way," I said as I pulled my shirt sleeve back to reveal the bite mark on my forearm.

161

Journal of Maya Weiss
November 14, 2013

Even ten days later, it's hard to even think about this, much less write it down. I was at Nate's house, during one of the seemingly endless planning sessions that had consumed my life almost from the day we arrived. Lynch and Shafer were debating something pointless, Nate was sitting back and listening while Dr. Shaked and Willie were consulting a book from the Heartland group's library. Just another day in post-apocalyptic America.

And then I heard my Amy's voice. I looked around, for some reason thinking she was in the room for a second before I realized it was coming from the radio room. Her first words are still ringing in my memory.

"Mom! Dave needs help!" she said. "Please, Nate, Mom, anyone. Can you hear me? Dave needs help."

I swear that room parted like the Red Sea. Half went for the radio, the other half went for the door. Shafer handed me the microphone the second I set foot in the radio room, and Amy told me what was going on. An army of zombies coming from the east, and Dave driving straight at them with the alpha zombie strapped onto his vehicle. He needed our help to stop them. Now it sounds so ludicrous. One man stopping an army with the help of a hundred other people.

Oh, and as an afterthought, the President was coming.

"Col. Shafer, I know you want to go help Sgt. Stewart, but there's nothing we can do. He's been bitten. It's just a matter of time, and you know he wouldn't want you to risk your lives on a fool's errand," the President said. I wasn't sure who she thought she was trying to convince. Shafer took the microphone from me, and he made me proud.

"Ma'am, you're probably right, he wouldn't want us to come help him, not against those odds. But you and I both know that's exactly what he would do in my shoes. Besides, he can't stop this mob on his own. Like it or not, we have to get out there." She didn't reply, and I was through waiting. I grabbed the mic from him.

"I'm coming, Amy," I told her. "Hang on."

"Roger that," I heard Nate say over the radio. I hadn't even heard him leave the room. "I'm on my way, kid."

"Stomper, rolling," Lt Kaplan echoed.

One after another, people chimed in. Karma One, Heartland, Zombie Stomper, and finally, Porsche added Landmaster One to the list when I slid into the driver's seat. Lynch said "Ooh-RAH Marines! Mount up!" as we headed for the gate.

We looked like hell. A hundred different vehicles with almost no discipline and no clue what we were doing. But I was damned if I was going to be behind anyone on this trip. Someone must have spread the word, because everyone got out of the way as I drove toward the head of the column.

We saw them a couple of miles north of the compound, a girl in a helmet with blue Mohawk streaks on a dirt bike, a black armored transport and a heavy truck. The truck kept going south, but the bike spun around and headed back to the east, and the armored car followed her.

There weren't many people here who didn't owe Dave their lives. He'd already done so much alone. But not today. Today, it was our turn to help him. Even if we couldn't save him, by God, he wouldn't die alone.

Chapter 10
The Last Mile
*~ Brotherhood means laying down your life for somebody,
really willing to sacrifice yourself for somebody else. ~ Tim
Hetherington*

The only good thing about facing an army of zombies is that
they're so damn slow. I was driving like a maniac, on the other
hand, or at least as crazy as I could in a massive armored vehicle
that couldn't beat seventy miles an hour. Up ahead, I saw the
Medicine Bow Mountains, and an idea took root in my head. The
far side was a relatively gentle slope up, but the side closest to
me was much steeper, with several vertical faces. As I came
around the southwest edge of the mountain range, I saw the sign
for Sugarloaf Mountain, and up ahead I could see its much more
modest profile across the lake in front of me. In better times, it
might have made a nice place for a wedding.

I pulled to a stop and checked the map. The road turned due
east just before Sugarloaf. The oncoming horde had to still be a
ways off, though I was starting to get that creepy vibe across the
back of my neck again. If they were still east of us and on 130,
this was going to be my spot. I took the left and turned past a
sign that marked the entrance to the Lookout Lake Recreational
Area. I stayed on the road until I hit the lake's edge, then I went
four wheeling, following the rocky western shore along until I
found a good spot. Above me, a narrow gap beckoned, though
narrow in geological terms was still big enough to drop a house
into. I pulled past the gap, then backed up the slope until I was in
between the base of the vertical faces. From here, I could see a
good ways down the road, and off in the distance, I could see the
zombies approaching.

Curious, I popped the gunner's hatch open and took a look
through the binoculars at the slow moving mass of dead people.
None of the ones I could see moved with the slow, shuffling gate
of the stage twos, the zombies. These all looked like ghouls.
They were faster, but easier to put down for a while. But after
that, it was a head shot or nothing.

"Have you turned yet, little monkey?" Bach asked from
behind me. "I don't think you have. I can still feel you there."

"Nope, still human," I said.

"It's only a matter of time," she said. "That little shot they gave you won't save you. Nothing can do that."

"It isn't supposed to," I said as I set the binoculars aside and opened the Mk 19's receiver. "It's just supposed to buy me a little more time." As I talked, I pulled the can of high explosive grenades out of the tray and reached for the HEDP rounds.

"Time? Why fight it? If you're going to die, just put a bullet through your head and be done with it. Why prolong it?" As she talked, I loaded the first round into the receiver and closed the top, then pulled the charging handle back.

"Why not?" I said as I pressed the butterfly switch and let the bolt go forward. The belt advanced the first round into the chamber, and I grabbed the charging handle and pulled it back again. "I have this thing against dying, but if I'm going to go out, why not go out like a boss? Warrior's death and all that." The fifty had a full can, so I ducked back down and pulled my M4, both Landry's P90 and mine, plus his Five-seveN. Finally, I pulled the Deuce's scabbard out. Amy had helped me strap it to the Ruger Takedown's carry bag to make it easier to get on and off in a hurry. I fully intended on going through every round I had with me and taking out as many as I could with the Deuce before they took me down or I went zombie. For good measure, I also grabbed a couple of fragmentation grenades from the ammo stores at the rear of the main compartment.

My right arm throbbed under the vambrace, and I wished I could scratch at the sudden itch that started around the wound. I consoled myself with the thought that I was going to be too busy killing infected soon to notice. That gave me a moment's pause. Was that the hyper-aggression from the Asura virus, or was that the zombie killer in me, the Nephilim blood in my veins that always seemed eager to kill zombies? Whichever one it was, I was going to make the best use of it I could. With a wistful smile, I reached for the iPod we'd found in Landry's pocket and plugged it into the exterior PA, then pulled myself out through the turret hatch.

"How did you turn Landry?" I asked Bach as I propped her up so she could watch me play havoc with her little army.

"I didn't, little monkey," she said with a cruel smile. "You did."

"I'm pretty much the opposite of one of you," I said. "So try again."

"Not you," she said with an exasperated head shake. "Your barely evolved simian race did our work for us. We could never have done it so quickly one bite at a time. Not even in your most crowded cesspits. But you...you devised an idea we would never have even thought of. You put it in your food!"

"Our food..." I said, my knees shaking as I planted my butt on the edge of the turret.

"That's right, monkey. The Asura isn't confined to bites or body fluids. You've been harvesting it in your crops and gorging yourself on your own extinction for months!"

"There's no way you could know that," I said.

"They kept the alpha from the first outbreak in Persia. He was there when Sikes first tried to harness the Asura in Nevada. What one of us knows, we all know. And now you're going to die knowing it was your own greed that killed your race."

"You're going to watch me kill a whole bunch of your kind first," I said. The zombie killing rage took enough of the edge off of the horror that threatened to shut my brain down to keep it at bay, and I climbed back into the turret. Below me, I could see the first of the infected moving through the valley made by two smaller hills. It was almost time to make my last stand.

I hit the play button on the iPod, and the first low knells of AC/DC's Hells Bells rang out across the lake. Landry might have been a dick when I knew him, but the man had good taste in music. I racked a round into the chamber on the fifty, then waited for the horde to get a little closer.

They barely seemed to be moving but after several minutes of waiting, the first of the horde hit the midpoint of the valley. That was when I pressed the trigger on the turret controls and sent the first tracer rounds toward the mass of once-human flesh. Hundreds of yards away, I could still see the results of the impacts as ghouls got tossed around like rag dolls. Fifty caliber rounds had originally been designed to shoot down armored aircraft. Against infantry, even undead infantry, it was devastating. The gun pounded in my ears, and I tracked the tracer rounds through the front ranks of the dead, sending bodies and parts of bodies tumbling with short bursts. After the first few bursts, though, the ghouls did what live soldiers would be hard pressed to do: they charged forward. I kept the trigger down for longer as I raked it across the thick wall of infected. More and more fell, but they reached the mouth of the valley and began to spread out, making it harder to slow them down. When the fifty ran dry, I could hear Bach cackling behind me.

Her laughter stopped when I hit the trigger control for the Mk 19 and traversed the turret across the front of the line at the lake's far shore. Five meter wide holes appeared in middle of the column, with wider gaps showing up on the outer edges. Even short bursts with HEDP rounds were far more effective than Ma Deuce's efforts.

"No!" Bach screamed from behind me as the line faltered for a moment.

"Welcome to modern warfare," I called out before I brought barrel back across the ghouls. More bodies went flying as another string of HEDP shells detonated among them. Movement to the west caught my eye, and I saw another group of ghouls come running along the outside of the westernmost hill. I turned back to look at Bach, and she bared her gray teeth at me in a hateful grin.

"Only a fool fights with the enemy general looking over his shoulder!" she crowed. I raised an eyebrow, stood and reached behind me. Her grin vanished when I grabbed the corner of her box and flipped her around so that the Plexiglas landed facing down. When I turned back, I saw that I'd caught a little bit of a break. The lake was slowing the ghouls in front down. The ones behind were starting to get backed up as the vanguard slogged across the bottom of the lake. Unfortunately, even with the rain from the night before, the lake was only a few feet deep. I didn't know if ghouls could swim, but since doorknobs were pretty much beyond them, I figured swimming would be too. Very few disappeared completely below the surface, and most of those tended to pop back up a few seconds later. But, it was still a slow walk across the lake. I walked the last few rounds in the can along a narrow spot in the lake, then grabbed another can of ammo for both guns.

As I racked the first round into the Mk 19 and pulled the charging handle again, I took stock of things. I hadn't expected to be able to reload, but I had hoped to do more damage by the time I ran out of ammo for the mounted weapons. The first of the soggy ghouls emerged as I primed the M2, and I let loose on them at closer range. This time, I could see the rounds hitting two and three of them at a time, the overpenetration knocking more of them back as they started to come across the rocky shoreline. But the line of them was too broad, and I couldn't stay ahead of them.

In the space between switching from the machine gun to the grenade launcher, they charged again. This time, Mother Earth herself was my ally. The spot I'd chosen made a deep V shape the further up the trail you went. Instead of spreading out, the terrain forced them back together into a wedge shape. Below, the rest of the ghouls were stacking up in an attempt to push their way into the narrowing ravine. Gravity worked against them, slowing their advance enough that I could take my time and walk my shots down the middle and along the sides.

When the first of them was about fifty yards away, I flipped Bach's case back over.

"What are you doing?" she demanded. Without a word, I traversed the turret right. The last notes of Hell's Bells faded, and the opening riff of Thunderstruck started playing. Just to be dramatic, I waited until the first chorus of "Thunder!" belted out of the speakers before I pulled the trigger. Four HEDP rounds slammed into the side of the mountain, tearing chunks of rock from beneath a sharp ridge. The cliff face seemed to shift, but not enough to satisfy me, so I pulled the trigger again. A low rumble started, and I turned the turret left. Once more, when AC/DC called out "Thunder!" I pulled the trigger, pounding the nearer cliff face with a longer burst. Chips of rock rained down on the Guardian as the belt ran out.

"Bringin' down the house!" I yelled over the growing rumbles of my artificial avalanche. Then I ducked into the vehicle as the left cliff face dropped more my way than I'd figured it would. Boulders rocked the armored sides of Guardian as the mountain fell down around me.

169

As soon as the world stopped rocking, I tried the upper hatch. It wouldn't move, so I tried the driver's overhead hatch. It slid aside with a shower of rock dust, and I emerged into the sunlight. The side of the mountain was now at the base of it, extending halfway through the lake. Most of the ghouls were buried under tons of rock, but that was a problem. Most of the ghouls still left a shit ton of them still up and walking around. The turret was bent all to hell, both guns pretty thoroughly destroyed.

It was time to get personal. The Asura-fueled aggression raging through my blood made that seem like the best idea I'd had in a long time. I ducked down into the vehicle and grabbed my guns and my sword, then crawled out of the hatch. As I slid the Deuce into its scabbard across my back, I heard rocks shifting nearby. I looked over the side to see Bach floundering beside the Guardian, her box shattered a few feet away. Long red scrapes ran down her explosed flesh, and I could see areas of dead flesh turning a mottled black on her arms.

"That's gonna leave a mark," I told her as I climbed along the top toward the rear of the ruined turret.

"Laugh while you can, Survivor," she snarled. "You'll be screaming sooner than you think." I didn't say anything as I crouched down on one knee and brought the P90 up.

Even after the avalanche, I had a target rich environment. Squeezing off short, controlled bursts, I went through the first magazine too fast for my taste. Ghouls dropped with every touch of my finger on the trigger, though. That brought a smile to my face. I changed out magazines in a few seconds and went back to shooting ghouls. They had advanced a little further than I'd wanted, so I flipped the selector to full auto and sprayed all fifty rounds in a sweeping, sustained burst that dropped most of the ones closest to me. Sure, they were going to get up again, but that wasn't happening for a little bit.

I dropped the last of my spare mags onto the P90 and tried to keep it more controlled, popping off short bursts into groups and bringing down four and five at a time. By the time that magazine ran dry, they were within a few yards of the Guardian, and it was time to get tactical. I dropped the first P90 and pulled the second one up from my side. I'd set this one to single fire, and every squeeze on the trigger sent blood flying and put another ghoul down.

When they got to the front of the vehicle, though, they didn't try to swarm up. Instead, they moved around to the side, and I realized too late what they're real objective had been. They weren't coming to get me.

They were after their boss.

Bach's cackle was like an ice pick on a chalkboard to my ears as they dragged her away. I stood up and shot as many of the ghouls nearby as I could, but I already knew it was too late. Several had thrown themselves on top of her, and even from more than twenty feet away, I could smell something putrid as the flesh slid off their bodies. Just to make her life difficult, I pulled one of the grenades from the pouch on my vest and flipped the safety, then pulled the pin and threw it at the writhing horde on top of Bach.

Once the spoon went spinning and Mr. Grenade was no longer my friend, I hopped off the left side of the Guardian and ducked down. Seconds later, there was a loud *boom!* and I could feel the pressure of the blast rock the Guardian. For what felt like an eternity after the grenade went off, my vision grayed and I couldn't tell up from down. As soon as I could regain my feet, I stumbled toward the front of the vehicle and checked my right side. Two ghouls, or at least most of them, came stumbling out behind me, and I emptied the last few rounds in the P90 into them, then let it go and unslung the M4. Bach was screaming behind me, and I really wanted to put as much room between us as I could. Downhill seemed to be the fastest way to do that.

Three ghouls scrambled up in front of me, and I brought the rifle up. *One- two, three-four, five-six* I counted as I popped two rounds apiece into them. They flailed as they went down and I kept going. A fairly healthy looking one jumped onto a car-sized chunk of rock in front of me, and I squeezed off three rounds to make sure it stopped being so healthy. It fell behind the boulder and I ran up the slight incline of the nearer face. About a dozen were climbing up out of the lake below me, but I could hear the slap of feet on stone from a *lot* closer behind me. I spun to see three more bloody ghouls trying to catch me, two on legs that bent in a couple of extra places. For those three, I took my time and put a round center mass in each one. Then I turned back forward and started shooting the ones getting out of the lake after their morning swim. At that range, I hit about half my shots, finally dropping ten of them by the time the firing pin hit an empty chamber. I changed mags as quick as I could while I looked for more infected to shoot.

An inhuman screech from behind me stopped me before I could go further, and I turned around to see what Sarah Bach had become. Her newly regrown arms and legs were a pinkish red color, and her hands were long and clawed. Her torso was a blackened monstrosity with open holes and gashes of red that were slowly sealing themselves. And set atop the abomination she had made of herself, her face was once again perfect and almost human except for the expression that stretched it into a rictus of hate. Shooting her wasn't going to do anything, but I still had one or two other options. Besides, she was out of ghouls on the upper slope.

I turned and jumped off the boulder I was on, then half-slid, half ran toward the lake shore. Only my gloves kept my hands from being shredded by the edges of the rocks that I used to keep my balance. A ghoul in an ICP T-shirt ran up to me as I stopped to regain my balance, and I gave her a shot to the face with the butt of the M4 before I spun it around and put a handful of rounds into her chest. Another was right behind her, this one a big guy in a garish fast food uniform. He was at point blank range by the time I got the barrel turned on him and pulled the trigger. More were coming up out of the lake, so I started on the ones closest to me, pulling the trigger as fast as I could, only sparing a single round where I could. When the mag was empty, they were too close to bother with reloading, so I dropped the M4 and drew the Five-seveN with my right hand and flicked the safety off. Firing right handed, I had to take three shots to hit the closest ghoul, even at thirty feet, so I moved it to my left and dropped the one behind it on the first shot. Shooting with my good hand, I made better use of the next sixteen rounds, firing, lining up the sights on the next target and pulling the trigger again. I only had to track back on a couple of them, and they dropped with the second round. Rock grated on rock behind me as the slide locked back, and I moved right while I dropped the empty and pulled a fresh magazine from the holster. The solid ground of the shore was only a few yards away, but those few yards were still covered in loose rock. I didn't dare take my eyes off my footing as I made my way to the smoother ground. I could hear water sloshing behind me as ghouls tracked my movement, and over that the snarls of the politician struggling to make her way to me.

Once my feet were on damp earth, I broke into a run for a few steps before I turned to see what was behind me. It was better and worse that I thought. Bach was forty or fifty yards up the slope, stumbling along on her new legs. But between her and me were dozens of ghouls, most of them in the water slogging at me. Decision time.

I flipped the safety and shoved the pistol into my pocket, then pulled the second and last grenade from its pouch. My head was pounding as I flipped the safety clip away, then pulled the pin with a yank that sent sharp pains up my right arm. I *really* wanted to fuck the alpha zombie's day up hard, but even with minutes left on my game clock, I wasn't about to give up a single second I didn't have to. The first of the ghouls made it to the shore ten meters away from me, and I threw the grenade a few feet in front of it, then turned and ran.

The kill zone on a standard issue fragmentation grenade is about five or six meters. The fragmentation zone is about three times that wide. I figured I needed to cover at least five or six meters in four seconds or less to have a snowball's chance in Hell of keeping my ass relatively intact. Ten steps would probably get me to a safe distance.

I made it eight before Mr. Grenade went boom.

On screen, explosions somehow send the heroes into this graceful looking dive. I just fell down hard on my face. My vision went white and I couldn't breathe for what felt like an hour, but when I rolled to my side, debris was still raining down around me. My ears started ringing as I staggered to my feet and reached for the Five-seveN, only to find my pocket empty. My hand dropped to the tactical holster on my left leg and found the reassuring grip of my SOCOM. As my eyes learned to focus again, and the blurry images in front of me went from a hundred or so ghouls to just fifty or so, I flicked the laser sight on and brought the gun up.

"Take my love, take my land," I belted out as I pulled the trigger the first time. "Take me where I cannot stand. I don't care, I'm still free!" I pulled the trigger with every word, for once making every shot count. "You can't take the sky from me…" I sang as the slide locked back. The reload felt smooth as silk as I took a few steps backward. Twelve newly dead ghouls lay in front of me, and several more were running up to take their place, some tripping over the half dozen or so floating in the water. As I brought the pistol up again, I started with the next verse.

"Take me out to the black, tell 'em I ain't comin' back," I sang as I pulled the trigger and dropped ghoul after ghoul. "Burn the land and boil the sea, you can't take the sky from me!" The slide locked back again, and I dropped the mag. As I slammed the next one home, the rest of the verses of the Firefly theme song came to mind, memorized and sung off key among a bunch of other Browncoats while I'd been in Iraq. There were five total, but most people had only heard the first two and part of the fifth that were played during the opening credits. A few of the dedicated Browncoats in my squadron, however, knew all five when we first deployed. By the time we came home, anyone who dared call themselves a Browncoat could sing them all on cue. I hadn't sung them in years, but it came back like it was yesterday.

"Leave the men where they lay," I bellowed as I started shooting the next group of ghouls. "They'll never see another day…" The knee deep water slowed most of them down enough that even at a full run, I was able to pick them off before they got to the shore as I walked backward along the muddy waterline.

I ran out of mags for the SOCOM before I ran out of verses to the song, so I finished with the 1911, dropping nine more as I reached the curve of the lake. A few steps later, I was at the eastern edge of the water, with ghouls wading through waist deep water on one side, and another group running at me along the southern shore. Bach was keeping her distance, and if my time hadn't been running out fast, I would have been a little worried. The last echoes of gunshots faded into the distance along with my defiant "And you can't take the sky from me!"

I released the slide on the forty five and holstered it. The first ghouls from the south side would be a little bit getting to me, and Bach was only now coming up with the idea to bring the ones already in the water to the northern side of the lake. Now that I was standing still, a world of hurt caught up to me. My head was pounding, my right arm felt like it was on fire from my fingertips to my shoulder. My right glove was torn, and I could see blood on my hand. For that matter, my right sleeve was dark almost all the way down. Sweat dripped from every inch of exposed skin, and I ached all over. Every breath felt like I had an anvil on my chest. My time was almost up.

If I had to go out, I was going to go out like a boss. My left hand went up and over my shoulder to the grip of the Deuce, and my blood slicked right hand pulled the Tainto into a point down grip. As the blades hissed from their sheaths, I tried to decide what song I wanted to sing for my last stand. Queen's Princes of the Universe seemed oddly appropriate, but it was better to listen to than to sing. No, if I was going to make my last stand with a sword in hand, there was only one song to go with.

"I sing here of a brotherhood as sharp as any spear," I sang. As the opening verse of "Bare Is the Brotherless Back" fell from my lips, I started to my left, running back along the northern shore of the lake. Bach stopped, and even from a hundred yards away, I could tell she was confused. With the bulk of her ghouls on the opposite side of the lake, she'd probably thought she was going to flank me with a faster force. Now, they were going to have to go even further to catch up to me, and all she had on her side of the water was a dozen ghouls that were spread out along the shore.

I might have been infected, outnumbered and doomed to fail, but I was still Dave Stewart. The alpha zombies all called me the same thing, and I'd said it of myself dozens of times. I was a survivor, I was *the* Survivor, and I'd be damned if I gave up before I dropped dead. And I'd take as many ghouls down as I could in the process.

One of the lessons Willie had taught me back in Kansas City was that in a field battle, the best way to fight a group was not to fight the group. Most fighters weren't as good at fighting in a unit as they were on their own, so they didn't coordinate their attacks or defend each other very well. So, when you faced a group of opponents, you stayed mobile and brought them down one by one. It worked on people pretty effectively. Against the infected, it was even better. I skewered the first ghoul through the chest and shoved him aside as I sang at the top of my lungs. Another one was a few steps behind him, and I ran at him. His arms came up to grab me, and I ducked under, stepped past him and slammed the Tainto between his ribs. The knife came free with a sucking sound as I moved to the next one, slashing it across the neck. It slumped to the right, revealing another one standing behind it, so I let my follow-through bring the blade up and twisted it to bring it back down across its throat. Two more were a couple of yards away, so I ran up and brought the Deuce across the back of the first one's leg, then stepped around it and chopped across the back of the other's neck before it could finish turning to face me. The second one flopped like a marionette with cut strings, so I went back to its flailing companion and laid the edge hard across its temple. Three blocked my way behind them. I flipped the knife for a better forward thrust and ran at them.

"Vivat the Blackstar!" I sang as I kicked the middle one, a tattooed hipster in the remains of a plaid shirt, square in the chest. The momentum of my kick left me standing between the other two, and I brought both weapons forward as I sang "Hurrah for Calontir! And Ansteorra!" Black gore sprayed as both points erupted from their backs. It took a moment to pull the blades free. By then, the last four were almost on me. I spared a split second to stab the hipster ghoul in the eye, then wiped the Tainto off on his shirt and sheathed it.

With the Deuce in a two handed grip, I ran at the last quartet. My first blow sheared the top of the lead ghoul's skull away. I let the swing drop low as I took a step to close with the second one, and gutted it, twisted the blade in midair and slammed it into the face of the third, then pulled it free and spun it over my head to shear through the neck of the fourth one.

"The Lion and the Falcon stand together o'er the foe!" I finished, standing only a few feet from Bach. A line of partially liquefied ghouls stretched along the beach behind her, and her arms and legs looked less raw, but they didn't look quite right.

Her limbs weren't the same length, and the shapes were off, like they'd been made by someone who didn't quite know how human anatomy worked. As we faced each other, I crouched down and wiped the Deuce off on the last ghoul's dress.

"You're dying, Survivor," she said with a hiss. Her voice sounded strange, like she couldn't quite decide on a signature tone. "You did all this for nothing." Her face creased into a smile.

"Maybe," I said as I struggled to rise again. My legs shook as exhaustion started to have its way with me. "Or, maybe," I panted, "I just wanted... to get closer... to you." I turned the Deuce in my hand so that the blade was facing me and ran my bloody right hand along the side, with my thumb resting lightly on the edge. Crimson smeared against the dark, acid washed metal as I gave my weapon one final caress.

"Did you think you'd die fighting us?" she asked with a cackling laugh. "We've already killed you, little monkey. All we need to do is wait for you to turn." I drew the Tainto again and held it down at my side, fighting to keep my grip on its blood-slicked grip. I watched in fascination as a line of crimson slid down the blade, then a single drop fell from the point.

"Actually, I thought I'd kill you before that happened," I said as I slowly caught my wind. She threw her head back and laughed at that, sending a shiver down my spine at the sheer inhuman glee in her voice.

"We are the Asura!" she said. "We can't die. You've tried before, and you failed. You...can't...kill us!" She reached out and grabbed me by the throat, then lifted me off my feet as her grip cut off my air.

I stared into her eyes, and saw something there that I wasn't supposed to. I wasn't seeing one alpha zombie in front of me. *All* of them were looking at me through her. Something deep in my brain understood exactly what I was seeing, even if I couldn't put words to it. I was staring into something ancient, something so malevolent that my sanity rebelled at its very existence. Whatever the Asura was, it was older than humanity, and it wasn't from around here. Its motives and where it came from were things I'd probably never know, and as I tore my gaze away from the horrors that lurked behind her soulless gaze, I knew I was happier not knowing. I only had one thing that kept me sane, and Bach or whatever was looking at me through her must have seen some glimmer of that knowledge, because her grip loosened enough for me to get a gasp of air into my lungs.

"What..?" they/it managed to get out before I brought the Tainto up and plunged it into the misshapen arm that was holding me up. She dropped me, and I fell to my knees as she staggered back, her other hand gripping the injured limb. My lungs expanded on instinct, drawing precious air down my burning windpipe. But as good as it felt to breathe again, I forced myself to look at where I'd stabbed her.

The wound was turning dark red, and the flesh around it began to pucker. Thin red lines began to appear under the gray flesh, slowly widening as they crept up her arm. She pulled the knife free and her eyes went to line of my blood that stained the blade as she fell to her knees.

"How?" she asked, her face suddenly expressing a new and alien emotion to her: abject terror. I pushed myself to my feet, my body trembling rom the effort. With shaking arms, I raised the bloody sword and spoke the only truth I knew.

"I'm Nephilim. Killing you is what I do." I grabbed the blade in both hands and raised it over my head.

"You won't survive this," Bach, or whatever was speaking through her said. I could see hundreds of ghouls emerging from the lake behind her, their legs splashing water as they tried to run.

"I might not survive," I said with a weak smile. "But I *will* win." With a final defiant yell, I brought the blade down on her skull with all my remaining strength.

I don't know what I was expecting when an alpha zombie died, but a surprised gasp sure as hell wasn't on the list. Maybe I'd hoped for something more spectacular, but I guess for something that never thought it could be killed, dying was something of a shock to it. I wrenched the Deuce free with the last of my strength, then staggered back. Behind her, the ghouls faltered and stopped. The world started to go fuzzy and bright around the edges, then I felt my legs give way, and I fell. I could feel my heart pumping fast in my chest, and there was a buzzing in my ears. I could see the ghouls closest to me start to move into my peripheral vision. My arms felt like they weighed a ton as I tried to reach for the Deuce.

The buzzing got louder, and one of the ghouls dropped to its knees beside me. Gray hands reached for me as it opened its mouth. Then there was a boom and its head just disappeared from the shoulders up. Another ghoul came closer, and its chest erupted before its head disappeared as well.

"Get away from him, you bastard!" I heard a familiar voice scream, and Amy stepped up. With one foot on either side of me, she pumped another round into her shotgun and fired again. More gunshots reached my ears, and more people joined Amy. Hernandez and Kaplan came up on her left while Nate Reid took a spot to her right. He'd grown in his beard but his dark hair was sill black and thick under his bandana. He brought a boxy SMG to his shoulder, and my brain put a name to it. *HK UMP* I thought as he fired it in tight bursts. Amy put the last round from her shotgun through a ghoul's chest, then drew her Browning and started shooting.

"Not today motherfuckers!" she yelled as she dropped ghoul after ghoul. "Not today!" More people joined them, and I saw familiar faces. Captain Adams and his team, Willie and his squad. If I could have screamed at them to get away, I would have. Right after I told Amy I was proud of her.

"Get him out of here!" Nate called back over his shoulder between shots. "Will, keep that right flank secure." He stepped forward and Amy moved with him. Gunshots came from behind them, and I heard Willie say "Thank you, ma'am!"

When Maya came to stand over me, I thought I was hallucinating. Porsche appeared to her left. Both of them were shooting to the side of the group, then they slung their weapons as another woman showed up wearing a tac vest and a helmet.

"I'll cover you!" the new woman said as she hefted a short M4.

"Porsche, grab his arm, Kaplan, take his legs!" Maya said as she knelt beside me and hooked her right arm under my left armpit. Porsche copied her move, and I felt someone grab my legs behind my knees. "Amy, with us! And…up!" Maya called out. I was lifted into the air, and my head fell back. In my upside down view, I could see two Strykers and a double handful of

Humvees pulled up at the edge of the lake. The woman in front of us turned and shot at a couple of ghouls that were coming up from the lake, and I could see a pair of white wings on the back of her vest. Then Maya's hand was on the back of my head, pulling me up to face her. "I've got you, baby. I've got you," she said as she carried me between two of the vehicles. Behind me, I heard Nate's voice calling out something, and people started running past us.

Then I was in one of the Strykers, being laid gently down. Another voice lifted above the sound of gunfire, and for a moment, silence fell. They were putting me in a small space with people. Not a good idea!

"Black Magic, what's your status?" I heard Nate's voice over the radio. Someone handed Maya a radio.

"I've got him," she said. "Precious cargo is secure, I mean."

"Roger that. Kill zone is clear. Rock and roll, boys and girls!" The roar of machine guns was drowned out by the Stryker's engine. The unknown woman grabbed something on my vest and then started pulling it off of me. Amy undid the gorget and arm protection like a pro, and then Maya was cutting the bandage free of my arm. As they worked, I felt the revolver slide from the holster, and I forced my hand to grab it.

"Amy," I rasped. Everyone froze. I tried to push the gun toward her, and she reached out for it. "Don't let me turn...not in here....please."

"Not today," she said as she took the gun from me. Tears ran down the side of my face, and I wasn't sure if it was from pain, pride or fear.

"She's right, Dave," Dr. Lennox said as Maya made room for him at my side. "If you were going to turn, you probably would have by now. It's just a matter of surviving the bite now..." The rest faded away as my eyes closed.

180

Chapter 11
No rest for the wicked
~ Death is a delightful hiding place for weary men. ~
Herodotus

"Good morning, little brother," Nate's voice reached my ears. I blinked sleep away from my eyes and inhaled the scent of coffee. I was in the guest room at Nate's place. The big bed was the most comfortable thing I'd felt in a month. On my right, an IV was hung from a stand, with a couple of machines that went ping beside it. Nate was sitting beside the bed with a white mug in hand and a faint smile on his face. "Looks like you decided not to die on us."

"Not yet. Can you inject a little of that in the IV?" I said as I pointed to the mug in his hand. He laughed and set the mug down. He wore a green flannel shirt open over a black t-shirt, with a pair of faded blue jeans. He shifted and I could hear the thick soles of boots on the floor.

"How you feeling?" he asked.

"Like every mile of bad road between Springfield and here," I said.

"You look it," he said, but most of the humor was gone from his voice as he leaned forward. "While we have a minute, and you can't defend yourself, I wanted to say thank you again for getting Cassie and Bryce out of Springfield."

"That was mostly Maya," I said but he shook his head.

"They told me what you did. You let yourself get captured to make sure they got away. Impressed the hell out of Adams. Shafer, too. Don't be surprised when they volunteer you to join the team."

"Dude, I'm not Special Forces," I said. He just gave an amused grunt.

"You're a hard core, zombie killing son of a bitch," he said seriously. "And right now, you're a god-damn hero to a lot of the folks here. Hell, Morris wants to pin a fucking medal to your chest for that dumbass move you pulled the other day. So don't think you're done just because you got here." He leaned back and glowered at me. I managed a weak smile.

"Bet she wants to give you one, too."

"Yeah, and I blame you for that. And your kid. God, don't get me started on her." He shook his head and rolled his eyes.

"That bad, huh?" I asked.

"Biggest damn case of testosterone poisoning I've ever seen." I laughed with him over that for a few seconds. "It ain't all parades and speeches, Dave. There's a group of folks who want to toss you over the fence because you were bit."

I tried to shrug. "Guess I should've expected that. Let me guess. People are starting to believe they're right?"

"Yeah, and we're going to have to get ahead of that somehow. But...not right now. Right now, you need to rest. And I need to wake my relief up." He got up out of the chair. My head felt heavy as I tried to lift it, but I managed to see the rest of the room for a few seconds. Nate was squatted down next to a cot on the far side of the room. Seconds later, Maya stood up and came over to sit on the bed beside me.

"Hello, sweetie," she said.

"Hello, sexy. I missed you." She leaned down and put her arms around me, and for a little while, that was all we could do besides kiss and murmur to each other.

"Amy said you had something you just had to ask me when you woke up," she finally said. "What's so important?" I ran my fingertips along the side of her face.

"Well, I kinda hoped to make a big production out of it," I whispered. "But...I made a promise to Amy when we crashed in Kansas City. And the whole way here, I kept wondering why it was so easy to make it. But, when I was driving toward that lake...the one thing I kept regretting was not asking you sooner."

"Asking me what?"

"If you'd be my partner for the zombie apocalypse. Be River to my Doctor, Irene Adler to my Sherlock Holmes..."

"Catwoman to your Batman?" she said with a smile.

"Why, Miss Weiss, are you asking me to marry you?" I asked.

"I don't think we have a lot of choice. Besides..." she kissed me. "It's mostly a formality by now. Everyone else calls you Amy's father, and she hasn't been telling anyone any different. I think a June wedding is too much to hope for."

"We'll be lucky to make it past Thanksgiving," I said. "Or did I sleep through that?"

"You were out for a couple of days. We almost lost you a couple of times the first day, but you spiked a fever last night, then it broke after a couple of hours. After that, you were just...asleep. The Ghostly Trio said you were probably suffering from exhaustion."

"The Ghostly Trio?" I asked.

"Our three doctors in residence. Your friend Dr. Lennox, Dr. Harris from KC and the president's virologist. They wear their lab coats all the time, and someone started calling them that. So, congratulations, you're the second person to survive a zombie bite."

"The second...so that's how you knew I wasn't going to turn. Who was the first?"

"Cheryl Carson. She got here a couple of days before you did. She was the one covering us when we dragged you away from the horde. But...we weren't sure if you would turn or not. She got bit a long time ago."

"In Nevada," I said, realizing I'd heard her last name before. "She was in Providence, during the second incident. The one I wrote about in The Frankenstein Code. But they never mentioned that she'd been bitten."

"She never mentioned it. She said it didn't seem important at the time. Anyway, even if you didn't turn, the bite still could have killed you."

"Not a chance," I said with a grimace. "That would have been too easy. But you know what I want right now, more than anything?"

"What's that?" Maya asked expectantly.

"Breakfast." I grabbed her for a kiss before I let her go. After she helped me sit up, she headed down to Nate's kitchen, leaving me alone for a few moments. Outside, I could hear vehicles running, the sound of people working on a hundred different things and life in general. People were building a life from the wreckage. For the first time since Zompoc Monday, I let myself hope a little. Maybe, I mused, we had a shot at making it through this.

Dear Readers,

Thanks for picking up Zompoc Survivor: Odyssey and joining me on Dave's latest adventure. I've been waiting for a long time to reveal some of the secrets of the Asura virus that Dave discovers here. Odyssey marks the end of the first chaotic stages of the zombie apocalypse, and the first hints of humanity's attempts at organization and recovery. As you can imagine, Dave's adventures are far from over.

I can't tell you how much I enjoyed writing Odyssey, and at the same time, how difficult some parts were to get through. Seeing Dave's relationship with Amy get stronger, and being able to give them some good memories in the face of world-ending horrors was also enjoyable. In the future, in addition to more of Dave's exploits, I'll be releasing the stories behind his two books, which will give you more of the background behind the world of Zompoc Survivor.

I always like knowing what my readers think, which is why reviews are so very important. Feel free to leave a review, and let your voice be heard. Or, you can leave a comment on my author page on Facebook. And, as always, come on by my website to keep up with the latest info.

In closing, I want to say thank you again for picking up Zompoc Survivor: Odyssey. You are the reason I write. While you wait for the next in the series, turn the page to check out more books from some other talented authors. And until next time,

Stay awesome,
Ben Reeder

FROM THE PAEAN OF SUNDERED DREAMS!

At the end of the world, one woman holds the only key to the future, written in madness and blood.

Fifteen years after the events in *Rationality Zero*, Earth falls to an apocalypse that none could have seen. In this whisper of a possible future, the worst nightmare of the Facility comes into being.

But is it true? Or are we simply peering into the mind of a deranged woman, who cannot tell fact from fiction?

In this odd story, which nestles uncomfortably into the timelines of **_Rationality Zero_, _The Herald of Autumn_, _Collateral Damage_,** and **_The Primary Protocol_**, Rational Earth falls to the darkness of the Shroud. Will our world recover from the desolation of darkness and madness that storms at the center of creation? Or, like the world of **Cæstre**, will all that man has wrought be lost?

None can say. Whether terrifying truth or irrational fantasy, one young woman holds the fate of all in her trembling hands.

What are people saying about "The Wormwood Event?"

One of the better short stories I've read in a while. Great flow throughout the story. I will definitely read more of this author.

185

This is a real chiller-thriller book. While you're trying to contain your shivers, your heart is thumping with the excitement of what's going to happen next.

This was my first time stepping into a world brought to life by JM Guillen and I am still in awe of his words.

This was my first experience of this author and I highly recommend him based on what I've seen so far.

<u>The Wormwood Event</u>

FIRST IN THE PAEAN OF SUNDERED DREAMS!

The world is not what it seems.

Michael Bishop has is an Asset of the Facility—a job that comes with many strange perks. He is a man who never gets ill, who never pays taxes. He is effortlessly fit, and has a different woman every night of the week.

That is, when he is not on assignment.

When activated, Michael becomes Asset 108, an enhanced human who stands against the strange darkness that lurks at the edge of our world.

Armed with equipment that most would find impossible to comprehend, he is sent on missions both strange and deadly. Each dossier pits him against irrational creatures and beings—most with the power to unravel his sanity, or reality itself.

It's never a simple job.

This one, however, is more complex than most. Mysterious unknown targets are fracturing reality, somewhere in the middle of the Mojave Desert.

The Facility has no other Assets in the area, and their telemetry is spotty at best. Without knowing what to expect, Bishop is activated, assigned to a cadre, and sent to the middle of nowhere.

What he finds there is both the beginning and the end.

Rationality Zero

63539122R00105

Made in the USA
Lexington, KY
10 May 2017